LETTERS OF FREEDOM

THE CARMEL SHEEHAN SERIES

JEAN GRAINGER

CHAPTER 1

*C*armel dusted the mantelpiece with the ridiculous purple feather duster Bill's twin daughters had given her for Christmas. Who on earth gave someone a duster as a gift, she'd wondered at the time, and she was none the wiser now. If they were little children, she thought maybe it could be explained, but that wasn't the case.

And while she wasn't materialistic at all, even she had to admit that one cheap plastic duster from the discount shop between two grown women was stingy. She'd never had a gift, not a proper one, ever chosen for her. To get something from someone, just once, that said 'I saw this and thought of you' would be lovely. Maybe Sinead and Niamh saw a plastic duster with bright purple feathers and thought of her. She didn't know which was a worse idea – that it was a thought-less gift or that they actually thought of her when they were in the home-cleaning section of Dealz.

They got her a blue scarf for her birthday each year. And Bill gave her twenty euro. No 'to my darling wife' card, not even a brown envelope, just a grubby twenty-euro note. Still, she thought, at least they marked the date. It was better than nothing.

When she was growing up in Trinity House, birthdays were avoided. It was a thorny subject, what with some children knowing

1

their stories and others not, so all birthdays were ignored. It seemed to be the fairest thing. She knew her birthday, the 21st of August – it was written on her birth certificate – so at least she had that. Not much else, mind you, but she fared better than some of the others. At Christmas they each got a stocking with some treats, but everyone got the same so there would be no arguing.

It was one of the many things she used to fantasise about as a kid, that someone would buy her a gift just for her, based on her likes or interests. And she'd foolishly thought that if only she had a family, then it would be a given. It was what families did, wasn't it? At least on television that's how it seemed. But that, like almost all of her assumptions about family life, was completely wrong.

Despite never getting anything she'd like from Bill or the twins, she'd scoured the shops each year on their birthdays and again at Christmas for something meaningful for each of them, though the girls had everything any woman could ever want and Bill had no hobbies and didn't care about clothes, so it was hard to come up with anything unique.

It didn't matter anyway; they barely looked at the carefully wrapped presents she placed beneath the Christmas tree. All the girls wanted was the substantial cheque from their father, handed over in a brown envelope, like a bribe to a shady politician, Carmel always thought. They kissed his cheek and pocketed the cheque and that was that. A few months into the new year, they usually got a new car or a new kitchen or something, and Carmel knew Bill had funded it.

For Christmas now she'd learned the best thing to do was to buy Bill a jumper in Twomey's in town, brown usually or some variation on brown. The early years when she'd tried to give him other things – nice shirts wrapped with bows or socks with funny slogans or after-shave – had just been excruciating. He had no idea how to give or receive a gift, and it left everyone feeling awkward. Not even she could get excited about a brown V-necked jumper, so it suited everyone.

While she got cash on her birthday – seventeen of them now spent in this house – at Christmas he usually got Julia to buy her a modest

2

voucher for Mullin's Electrical in town. It sold some homewares too, so he probably assumed she'd get a few cushions or something. He never asked what she got with the voucher, and she never said.

As Bill handed over his hard-earned money to his grasping daughters each Christmas morning after Mass and before dinner, his expression came as close to pleased as she would see again for another twelve months. She wondered how that cold, loveless gesture of handing over a cheque in an envelope could make him happy, but it seemed to. Well, not happy exactly – that was an emotion very far from his repertoire of feelings – but pleased, proud maybe. It was impossible to know. Like everything else about her husband, how he felt was a total mystery.

She knelt down to dust the fireplace. The range in the kitchen was always lit, and this fireplace was only used on special occasions; to date there had been two. They'd had a Station, when Father Linehan said Mass in the house and everyone from their part of the parish came, and the night Niamh got engaged to Killian and his parents came over for a glass of sherry.

The Station had been agreed to under extreme duress, but it was their turn and eventually it had become too embarrassing to refuse to host it. Julia had been thrilled when Bill finally succumbed to the none-too-subtle hints of the parish priest, and she had gone into full hostess mode. Carmel was sidelined completely.

The engagement night was toe-curlingly embarrassing, as Killian's parents stood there, saying nothing, and Bill found successive excuses to go out to the farm. Killian did his best, but his father was another version of Bill and his mother was a tiny birdlike woman who looked permanently startled.

Carmel stood up and stretched her back, catching a glimpse of herself in the mirror over the fireplace, which had been given by some aunt of Gretta's as a wedding gift years ago. It was oval and had some odd bits of white curly metal all around the outside. It was an ugly thing and had become spotted with age, but like everything else, it had to stay exactly where *she* put it. Carmel once dared suggest that the awful orange and brown wallpaper in the living room be removed and the whole place painted a nice bright pastel, and Bill's face told her all she needed to know about that suggestion. The entire house was not just a shrine to Gretta but a study in the '70s: lots of orange and brown, Formica, beauty board, a swirly patterned carpet, a corduroy three-piece suite in a dull green. It was like a time warp, dating from even before Gretta's time. She must have had a thing for that garish look. It reminded her of the house in the television programme, The Brady Bunch. She and the other kids in the home liked to watch it, a perfect, happy family. Funnily enough, Carmel felt no ill will towards her predecessor. It was probably quite fashionable décor back in the day, and some of her clothes, still hanging in the wardrobe upstairs, were actually very stylish.

Carmel tucked a stray brown hair behind her ear; it had come loose from her ponytail. She was probably too old for long hair anyway. Perhaps Julia was right and it would be better short, but she'd lost her nerve after making the appointment and came home again, her shoulder-length mousy-brown hair untouched.

She'd scrubbed the oven earlier and there was a smudge on her cheek that she wiped with the hem of her apron as she paused to take in her reflection. She didn't generally spend too much time looking at herself. Vanity was frowned upon in Trinity House, as was seeking 'notice' or having 'notions'. Blend in, don't have ideas above one's station, tread lightly on the earth, speak quietly and rarely – those were the messages they got. The spotlight was not for children like her, with no past and no future. Try not to take up too much space; that was meant for other people.

She'd managed that much at least. She did blend in. Forgettable was how she looked, she decided. Not awful looking, not pretty either, just a middle-aged woman, medium height, medium build. Nondescript. The kind of person they used in those crime reconstructions on television. She'd be an ideal mugging victim, or the woman behind the main character in the queue at the checkout. A body, but not one anyone would notice. She could imagine the casting agents wanted an ordinary-looking woman to be a nobody. She smiled at the thought. At least she found herself funny; nobody else did, but she amused herself most days with her mad ramblings. She'd learned to live inside her head almost all of the time.

She came to the photo, just as she did every day. She didn't dare lift the large Waterford Crystal frame, afraid she would drop it, instead dusting around it so carefully. Bill and Gretta beamed out at her as they had done every day of her seventeen-year marriage. Her husband was dressed in his best suit, standing proudly beside the now deceased Gretta, who looked so young and innocent in floor-length white lace. The veil on her head looked old-fashioned now, but Carmel was sure it was all the go back when she and Bill got married. They looked so in love, so full of hope. Gretta was really pretty, Carmel thought. Her big brown eyes were so trusting as she gazed lovingly at Bill; her dark hair curled gently down her back. She reminded Carmel of a picture she'd seen of Gina Lollobrigida years ago, though without the huge breasts.

She remembered years ago there were some young men working on the new shower blocks of Trinity House, and one of them had a magazine and was showing the other men a picture in it. Sister Kevin appeared out of nowhere and caught them ogling the picture. She berated them for bringing such filth into the children's home and confiscated the magazine, as if the crew of builders were errant ten-year-olds, with dire warnings that she would report it to the foreman.

Kit, Carmel's friend, had been sent to Sister Kevin later that week for some transgression – impossible to remember which, as Kit was always in trouble – and she swiped the magazine from the desk drawer when the nun was called out. Carmel and Kit and few of the others had been astounded to see photographs of very scantily clad women.

Carmel never told Bill who Gretta reminded her of, but she remembered thinking that Gina Lollobrigida was one of the most beautiful women she had ever seen in her life. The girls didn't take after Gretta really – well, perhaps a bit, but they lacked their mother's vulnerable allure.

Carmel frequently caught Bill staring at the photo as he shovelled his dinner wordlessly down his throat every evening after milking.

Though he looked nothing like the open-faced smiling young man in the picture, his eyes were the same; however, the pain of his grief was still there. The initial agony he must have felt had dulled to an empty unfillable void, but Carmel knew that Bill missed his first wife every single day since cancer took her away from him and his little girls. Carmel was no substitute and never would be, no matter how hard she tried.

CHAPTER 2

*A*nd Carmel tried so hard in the early years, making nice dinners, keeping the house spotless. She even tried to 'spice things up in the bedroom', following to the letter the instructions in *Cosmo*, but nothing worked. She would take to her grave the look of perplexed horror on Bill's face that night in the first year of their marriage, when he came upstairs to find the bed scattered with rose petals, candles burning everywhere, and Carmel reclining, in what she hoped was a provocative way, in a new cream silk nightie. He just stood there for a second, looking appalled, and then muttered something about a sick calf in the shed that he needed to check on. By the time he got wordlessly into the bed beside her an hour later, she was in flannel pyjamas buttoned all the way up to the neck and all traces of flowers and candles gone. It was never mentioned by either of them again. She burned with shame whenever she thought of it – another failure.

That side of the marriage never existed. She had been dreading it, not having the faintest idea what to expect, and during the first nights was relieved when he put out the light and simply fell asleep. But as time went on, she knew they should be doing *something*. But he never seemed to have any interest. He never touched her, even inadvertently. It seemed strange at first to live beside someone, sleep in the same bed as them for so many years, and never touch, but now it was second nature. Nothing. Never a brush of a hand, a peck on the cheek, let alone anything more intimate. The years passed, and after that one mortifying incident with the candles and rose petals, the subject was never raised again.

She once or twice fleetingly played with the idea of asking him why he never wanted to do anything. She wondered if she was doing something wrong. She was bewildered as to why on earth he wanted to marry her in the first place. If all he wanted was a housekeeper, he could have employed someone easily enough. But she never had the courage to speak up.

Even the most innocuous of conversations seemed impossible. He didn't confide in her about anything, never had, so asking him about their marriage – or non-marriage really – would only embarrass them both. She didn't think it was because of the age difference, even though she was only forty to his fifty-four; it was more that they were totally incompatible. She loved people and chatting, and Bill was so quiet. He rarely spoke to anyone – it wasn't just her – and when he did, his words were economical, delivering information only.

'The spuds are going to be ready in around ten days, so I'll have some sent up,' had been this morning's only communication.

He'd get out of bed on his side the second the ancient alarm clock went off. He'd be up and out milking before she got up. But he'd return, having attended to the herd, and expect his breakfast. She always woke with the alarm too – it was impossible not to as it was so loud – but they never acknowledged each other. She would have liked one of those clock radios that woke you to some cheerful voice or a song, but that would have been another of her ludicrous suggestions. Instead, they had the loud 'tick, tick' all night and the horrible sound when the little metal hammer battered the bell on top of the brown clock. More brown. She'd never seen a brown alarm clock for sale – even the old-fashioned ones were red or blue or even pink – but Bill managed to procure a brown one.

'Do you think it will be a good crop this year?' she'd asked, trying to extend the only conversation with another human, apart from Julia, that she would have all day.

Bill made a sound that she took to mean 'I don't know' and stood up, shrugged on his jacket that smelled of sour milk from the dairy and left for the farm. No 'have a nice day, dear' or 'what do you plan to do today, Carmel?' or even a 'thanks' for the creamy porridge, grilled rasher and home-baked soda bread he had eaten for breakfast. He saw his role as farmer and provider, hers as cook and cleaner. And she was sure that to Bill's way of thinking, she should not be thanked for doing her job, any more than she should be thanking him for milking the cows.

The nuns had sometimes accused her of having an overly romantic idea about life outside the walls of Trinity House, and she had to concede they were right. Life was drudgery, no matter where you lived it.

She wiped a speck of dust from the frame with her thumb. Three decades had passed since the day Bill married Gretta. His dark curly hair was grey now, and the lean young farmhand had become a paunchy middle-aged farmer. But it wasn't just the time that had changed him. People in town had said to her that the day Gretta died, a bit of Bill died as well. Some people said it to be kind, she supposed, to try to explain that his taciturn nature wasn't her fault. She'd had to listen to how charming he was as a young man, how chatty and genial. It was hard to believe that at least some people did not in some way blame her for the transformation.

She had no idea what he was like before, but for the seventeen long years that she had known him, he was undoubtedly the most uncom-municative man in Ireland. His awful sister, Julia, was the worst for reminiscing about the old Bill. She exclaimed – as often as she could, as loudly as she could, to as many people as she could – how Bill was so much happier before. The before, of course, referred to 'before Carmel'.

As feelings of bitter hatred for her sister-in-law threatened to rise up within her, Carmel tried to think good thoughts. 'Challenging interpersonal relationships are a great opportunity to practice your mindfulness.' She quoted her self-help CD through gritted teeth. Bill never saw her Wayne Dyer or Deepak Chopra books and CDs; she kept them out of sight. Not that he'd say anything, but he'd get that look, the one that spoke volumes, the one that said, 'Gretta wouldn't be sucked in by all that hippy nonsense.'

The look of disappointment on Bill's face was a regular feature of her life; in fact it was one of the few emotions he expressed perfectly. So she kept her interest in mindfulness and gratitude and trying to live her best life to herself. At night she listened through her earphones to Dr Wayne Dyer's lovely deep voice in a podcast about drawing positive energy to you as Bill snored rhythmically beside her. If he noticed, he never once asked what she was listening to. In a way she was glad; it was her thing. Louise Hay, Dr Dyer and so many others made her feel less alone. The guided meditations that led her to places of calm, serene and stillness were the highlight of her day.

She had the internet on her phone, and she was in lots of Facebook groups, people united by the teachings of the New Age movement. One in particular she really enjoyed was set up to discuss the teachings of Dr Dyer. It was based in the UK, and the people on it were so nice and talked so much about positivity and love and service to mankind; she felt good being around them, even if it was only virtually. Though the ideas discussed were exactly the teachings of Jesus Christ she'd learned as a child – kindness, empathy, compassion, gratitude, love – this interpretation sat more comfortably than the strict rules and dogma of Catholicism.

She'd always felt an inherent threat in the faith of her childhood – do it the right way or face the fiery pit of hell. So much of the imagery even was terrifying. She recalled a particularly grotesque representation of Jesus's face on the Shroud of Turin, since debunked of course, that hung over the blackboard in one of the classrooms. Try as she might, age seven or eight, to not look at it, it drew her gaze and she couldn't help it. Poor Jesus, with the thorns pushed into his head – it used to make her cry. The saints and statues represented in every corner and wall of Trinity House shared the same expression – profound sadness.

She wondered at a faith that rejected joy so universally. The message seemed to be life was a trial of pain and suffering and if you endured it well, then when you died you got to go to heaven. But if not, your fate was an eternity of hell. And the opportunities for sin seemed everywhere, impossible to avoid. Kit used to joke as they came out of confession each Saturday that it might be best if she was hit by the number 78 bus right then, while she was in the clear, because sure as anything her soul would be filthy black and full of sins again by the morning.

The ridiculousness of little children being terrified of committing sins was obvious to her now at forty, but as a child she seemed to spend her whole life trying to avoid sin and failing miserably.

Then she found this new way of thinking, that she wasn't bad by virtue of just being, that she had a purpose, that God loved her and that she was a good person just as she was. This was a revelation and she loved it.

She found so many people in this new tribe; they were her only friends. Her name in the group was 'CarmelIreland'. She'd log in most mornings, and instantly someone in the group would send her a smiley face or a wink, or a 'Good morning, CarmelIreland!' post. For the first time in her whole life, she felt welcome and that she belonged. She found herself commenting on posts and revealing more about herself to these strangers than she ever did in real life. Just a week ago a person said how sad he was to discover posthumously that the man he thought of as his father wasn't in fact his natural father at all. The man said he felt betrayed and hurt that his father could never tell him the truth. Carmel felt compelled to tell her own story, and commented how being a parent was so much more than biology. Her birth parents had abandoned her in 1976, leaving her nothing but her name. She'd never known the love of a mother or father. She mentioned how he should try not to see it as a betrayal and instead more look at it that the man was his father, in every way that mattered. The conversation went on, with the original poster asking her about her childhood, and it felt nice to talk, even if it was electronically with someone she'd never met.

Whatever about Bill – he didn't seem to care what she did. But she could never let old hatchet-face Julia see what she was up to on Facebook. Julia would have her committed to the county home as a nutcase or bring her down to the priest to be exorcised. Mobile phones, computers – any technology past a pop-up toaster was, to Julia's mind, the work of the devil. And as for connecting with strangers online and discussing matters existential with them, well, that was surely a most grievous sin. As far as Julia was concerned, there was only one place for faith or spirituality and that was up at Mass every Sunday morning. Anything else was heresy.

Julia. The thought of her gave Carmel a stomach ache, which was ridiculous, as Carmel was a grown woman and should not be afraid of another one. But the truth was that she felt nothing but terror in her sister-in-law's company.

Carmel always thought of sisters, and by association sisters-in-law, as lovely, benevolent forces for good in a person's life. As a child, she'd devoured novels in which sisters and brothers and cousins solved mysteries or went on adventures, and she longed, more than anything, for a family herself, one of her very own. When she married Bill, with nine-year-old twins Sinead and Niamh, she thought she was getting just that, but from the very first day when Bill brought her to this house and she met her stepchildren and sister-in-law, Carmel knew something was very wrong. It was not like any book she'd ever read. The children were not timid exactly, more standoffish, like they didn't want her there, and Julia was openly hostile. Carmel was not a welcome addition to the sad little household of Bill Sheehan and his lost girls.

Carmel had never understood Julia. Bill's sister had apparently been the one who encouraged her brother to remarry, and yet she seemed to hate his new wife on sight. Julia talked constantly about Gretta, about how nice she was, how kind, how funny, how well dressed, and when she really wanted to put the boot in, how much Bill and the twins adored her. Carmel knew perfectly well that her husband didn't love her – he probably didn't even like her very much – and while she had sadly come to accept that fact, it wasn't nice to have her nose rubbed in it almost daily when Julia found a reason to 'pop in'.

CHAPTER 3

*C*armel was lost in her reverie, and she started as the clock struck the hour. It was only one o'clock. She tried to breathe, berating herself for her jumpiness. Nothing bad was going to happen. Julia was at work; as principal of the local national school, she never left before 4 p.m., so the chances of her 'popping in' before then were zero.

She glanced around the familiar house. Even if anyone did call, nothing was amiss. Everything was exactly as it should be, exactly as it was since the day Bill and Gretta first decorated it. Carmel remembered the first time she saw Bill's house, surrounded by a little flower bed and a neatly clipped lawn. She remembered her heart soaring as Bill pointed it out to her on the drive up the hill out of the town of Ballyshanley. She would never forget the sensation of relief and sheer joy – a home of her very own at long last. She'd practised saying 'my house' and 'my home' in her head and imagined scenarios where she was giving directions for deliveries or callers or proudly telling someone her address.

It was to be a short-lived happiness, but she still remembered that feeling, like everything was going to be OK. In the beginning, she imagined adding her own little touches, but very early on Bill said he wanted nothing changed, and he meant nothing at all, not the blue candlewick bedspread or the oil painting of the fields with the carthorse or the little crinoline lady that was to be placed over spare toilet rolls in the avocado-coloured bathroom for fear a guest should see them. Carmel cleaned the house and cooked in it – she even did the garden – but it was Bill and Gretta's house, not Bill and Carmel's. Julia pointed that out frequently.

Carmel sighed, thinking of her witchy sister-in-law. She was all pointy and thin, exactly like a witch in a story, and her dark hair was pulled back into a severe bun. She reminded Carmel of the witch with the green face in *The Wizard of Oz*. She was terrifying in every way. Carmel's heart went out to the little kids who had to have her as headmistress. Julia had taught at St Joseph's primary school since leaving university, working her way up the ladder to principal over years. She saw herself as a leader of the community, a keeper of standards and the authority on who belonged where. Carmel hated to hear her asides about the various families as she recounted events of the day to Bill. 'The Hartnetts out the valley road, sure every last one of them is an alcoholic,' or about the McDonaghs, 'The mother there is mad, you know, had to be sectioned in the end.' Julia hadn't a kind word for anyone. She admired the Desmonds because Daniel Desmond was the doctor, as was his father before him, and she was forever going on about the Harte family who lived in Hazelbrook House and were absolutely loaded with money. For a woman who called other people gossips and who quoted the Bible, she was never done passing judgement on others. Local gossip said it was because she had a notion for one of the Wootons, big local landowners, but he was only toying with her and dropped her for the daughter of the local Protestant gentry.

Julia claimed she never had time for marriage, and then when poor Gretta passed away so young, she knew that Bill and the twins needed her. She spun this story so often to anyone who'd listen, Carmel could almost recite it by heart. Subtext – they still needed her as his new wife had turned out to be such a disappointment.

Julia had several favourite topics, and Carmel could almost recite them by heart. In her mind she called them 'Julia's Greatest Hits'. Track one, the riff-raff that had come to Ballyshanley when they built the new council estate. Track two, the new curate was too familiar with people. Track three, Gretta was the love of Bill's life. Track four, Niamh and Sinead adored her, and although she was no substitute for their dear departed mother, she did her best. It went on and on.

The twins' graduation photo stood proudly beside their parents' wedding one. Sinead and Niamh were identical, and even after all these years, Carmel regularly let herself down by calling Sinead 'Niamh' or vice versa. Only their mother, Bill and Julia could tell them apart, another jibe from her sister-in-law. They were nice enough girls – Carmel tried to be fair – but they missed Gretta and never wanted a new mother; that much was very clear. She'd lost count of the number of times over the years she'd tried to engage the girls in activities or outings so that they could get to know each other, as all the parenting books she bought insisted was vital. Each time she tried, though, her offers were rebuffed, and Julia swept in, suggesting some-thing much more *appropriate,* as if Carmel wanted to take them to a lap-dancing club or to a rave. Carmel gave up eventually – another failure.

They were both up in Dublin now, Sinead working as an adminis-tration manager in Dublin Airport and Niamh expecting her first child – she was on maternity leave from some IT company in Dublin – a honeymoon baby after the wedding of the century.

Carmel's cheeks blazed at the memory of Bill's speech the day Niamh married Killian. For a man unaccustomed to speech, he really spoke eloquently that day about how proud Gretta would have been, how lucky they were to have her for the years that they had, how tragic her loss was for the whole family. There was a photo of her at the top table, and when Bill spoke, his eyes were firmly fixed on the photograph and suspiciously bright. He never referred to Carmel, or even looked in her direction. Sinead, the chief bridesmaid, wiped her eye, not wanting to smudge her carefully applied make-up, while Niamh's new husband squeezed his bride's hand reassuringly.

Bill raised a toast. 'To Gretta,' he said, his voice choked with emotion.

At least the guests had the good grace to look mortified, some even throwing her a pitying glance. Carmel got no mention in any other speeches either, even though she made the cake and the flower girl dress. The bride and bridesmaid and their Auntie Julia had gone to New York to go wedding-gown shopping. It never occurred to them to ask Carmel. She remembered how foolish she felt because she'd got a passport specially. Having never left Ireland before, she didn't have one. She used the special service in the post office, so everyone in Ballyshanley knew she got a passport thanks to Betty Big Mouth, the postmistress, and further embarrassment ensued when she wasn't asked to go on the big trip.

Ronan Collins came on the radio. He was her favourite DJ, and she loved his programme; he played all the songs she adored, not the really old stuff that Bill liked but songs from the '70s and '80s. Sometimes she talked back to Ronan when he spoke. If Bill heard her, he'd be horrified; he'd think she was bonkers as well as unlovable. But it was nice to have someone to talk to, even if he was on the radio and had no idea that Carmel Sheehan existed quietly in the town of Ballyshanley, Co Offaly. She'd smile when she heard Ronan wish someone a happy anniversary or say someone was eighty years young that day. She always imagined the DJ as a bit of a rogue, a charmer, and she wondered what he was like in real life.

She used to dream that one day she'd hear Ronan say, 'And now I have a request here for Carmel, whose birthday it is today, from her loving husband, Bill, and her daughters, Sinead and Niamh.' But she never dreamed of that any more. She even thought once about sending in a text to the show on her birthday to wish herself a happy birthday but stopped herself. That really would be barking mad.

She finished dusting and checked the fire surround for any specks of ash. It was set with paper and sticks, with the coal strategically placed on top 'for maximum chance of combustion'. She smiled at the phrase; Sister Kevin used to say that when they were lighting fires in Trinity House.

She wondered how things were there now. In the seventeen years since she'd left, there must have been a lot of changes. The older nuns had probably died or retired. *Just as well*, she thought. They were of a different time. There were so many rules and regulations now about children in state care. It was necessary, of course, as awful things happened to kids over the years in homes just like Trinity House, but she hated hearing stories of how horrific things were for people in institutions. She switched off when such tales came on the radio, not because she didn't care but because she wanted to say that not everywhere was like that. Trinity House had been devoid of love, that much was true, but she hadn't been abused by anyone. The nuns were all right, most of them, though one or two were very enthusiastic with the metre stick. Each school had been given a metre stick when they changed over to the metric system from the imperial one of feet and inches, but the rulers were put to a more creative use by one or two of the sisters. But she'd survived it and it really wasn't that bad. The worst part was feeling like she was a nuisance, a person to be 'dealt with' rather than loved and cherished. Her heart went out to the victims of child abuse in all its forms. She could hear the pain in their voices and saw the innocent little boys and girls these men and women once were. How people were allowed to get away with it hurt and angered her, but it was not her experience.

Julia had popped in last week and more or less asked her straight out if she had been abused. 'I'm so tired of all this whining on the radio, these so-called victims,' the witch announced as she made herself at home. 'I mean, look at you, for example – were you abused? Your mother, the misfortunate wretch, had you in a home for fallen women, and you ended up in an orphanage, reared at the cost of the taxpayer, and nothing happened to you, did it?'

Carmel was mortified, but she mumbled an agreement and gave Julia her cup of tea.

Trinity House was good – not as good as a home and a family of one's own of course, but good enough. The nuns who ran it were kind and they did their best. The day she left to get married, she was happy and sad at the same time; she was leaving the only home she'd ever known. She remembered Sister Margaret saying, 'Your mother would have been very proud of you, Carmel,' as she walked with the nuns to the chapel down the street from Trinity House in the beige skirt and jacket she had found in a charity shop and altered to fit.

Sister Margaret was just being nice – nobody had the faintest clue who her mother was, and whether or not she would have been proud of her daughter on her wedding day was a mystery – but it made Carmel feel a bit happier anyway.

The wedding was nice, the Mass said by Father Tobin, and he was so kind and funny. Afterwards the nuns put on a nice spread in a room off the community hall. Nobody was there from Bill's side – Julia stayed in Ballyshanley to mind the girls – and the witnesses were Sister Kevin and the sacristan, Mr O'Neill. Carmel remembered poor Sister Margaret and Sister Bonaventure trying to keep the conversation going over tea and sandwiches – they'd even made a little wedding cake – but Bill agreed with everything they said and contributed little else. After an hour, he put Carmel's small suitcase in the boot of his car and off they drove to Ballyshanley to begin their married life. Not a word passed between them on the journey. She'd known from the few meetings they had before the wedding that he wasn't what you'd call chatty, but she supposed it must have been hard for him to remarry and he would need time to adjust. She had been so wrong, though; he never did adjust.

CHAPTER 4

*C*armel considered running around with the Hoover one more time but there was no need; the place was spotless. She looked around at the dated furniture in the sitting room. How she hated that sofa. She would have loved to go up to Dublin and go into Hickey's Fabrics and buy material and make curtains and covers for the couch. She was very good with a needle and thread and had made most of her own clothes in Trinity House from other people's hand-me-downs. The nuns said she had a gift for needlework.

Not that the interior design of the house mattered really, she supposed. Nobody ever saw it except Bill, Julia and the girls. She had tried to make a few friends in Ballyshanley at the start, joining a book club and the church flower committee, but Bill didn't encourage it.

'I don't want the whole parish traipsing through here, nosing at what I've got,' he decreed, giving her that disappointed look again at the stupidity of someone even suggesting such a thing.

Julia dismissed her newfound social group too, claiming, 'They are only trying to find out about you – people love a sob story. And Gretta used to do the church flowers. Oh, she had such an eye for colour! Her May altar was the talk of four parishes! So it would be best not to try to usurp her memory. And sure, growing up in that place in Dublin, I doubt you know much about flowers and such like.'

And so Carmel bowed out, not wanting to look like she was trying to replace Saint Gretta. Soon after, she stopped attending the book club too because the arrangement was that the members had to take turns to host the meetings. Bill would have had a blue fit if she had anyone into the house to sit around drinking tea and talking about books.

She checked the clock again. Bill was meeting somebody from the Irish Farmers' Association that day to discuss compensation for the flooded fields of last winter, so he wouldn't be needing his dinner at one thirty like he usually did. She had until at least six o'clock that evening before he'd be home.

She thought that perhaps she'd tidy the shelves in the back kitchen. They were tidy enough, but maybe they could use a dusting. As she returned to the kitchen to fetch the bucket and a damp cloth, her phone pinged. The ringtone was for messages, and she rarely got any. Feeling a thrill of excitement, though it was probably someone spamming her to sell something, she took her phone from her pocket and swiped up to open the Facebook private message.

Dear Mrs Sheehan,

I hope this message finds you well. I also hope it doesn't come as too much of a shock to you. I have been trying to find you for many years. Your post on a page on Facebook pertaining to the American Dr Wayne Dyer seemed to indicate that you might be who I am looking for. I can't be sure, of course, and you may have some other information that could confirm or refute it, but your name and the dates are correct. To add to that, I had a look at your profile picture, and you do look very like her. I believe your mother – your birth mother, I mean – was a lady called Dolly Mullane. She passed away two years ago, I'm sorry to tell you, but she asked me to help her find you. She spent her entire life looking for you, and I can't tell you how sad I am that she didn't live to see you again.

My name is Sharif Khan, and I run a nursing home called Aashna House in Bedfordshire, England, where your mother spent her final years. Though I was her physician, she was also my mother's closest friend and I knew her my

whole life, long before she came to stay at Aashna House. She was a charac-
ter, to say the very least, and I would love to tell you about her.

I do not know if you would like to meet me, or if I have anything to offer
except to tell you of your mother, but if you would like to, I will be in Dublin
on the 9th of April. I will stay at the Gresham Hotel, and I will be in the lobby
at 2 p.m. I will wait until 2:30, and if you do not arrive, I will assume you do
not wish to have any contact with me. I bear no bad news, Mrs Sheehan, but
I have some photographs and some correspondence from your mother that I
would dearly love to deliver to you.

I hope to see you on the 9th.
Yours sincerely,
Sharif M. Khan

Carmel stared at the screen, her mouth dry, her heart thumping.
Today was the seventh. The ninth was in two days' time. What if it
was a scam? People were always saying how the internet was full of
charlatans and criminals. But why would someone do this? She had
no money and she wasn't an important person, so what was in it for
this Sharif Khan?

She read and reread the message over and over. She checked out
his profile, which was private. She considered sending a friend
request but baulked at the last minute. She googled Aashna House. It
was a hospice in Bedfordshire, England, as he'd said. She looked at the
gallery and saw his picture. Dr Sharif Khan was handsome, dark
skinned, with dark, almost black, eyes. He was dressed in a grey suit
and wore a white doctor's coat. She swallowed. She'd never spoken to
a real doctor in her life. She'd gone to the nurse in the local practice
once or twice, but she was remarkably healthy and had never had
need of old Dr Cotter. She used a lot of natural medicine, preferring
to deal with any ailments that way.

Could it be that Sharif Khan really did know her mother? The
words swam round in Carmel's brain – her mother, her mother.
Normally she didn't allow her mind to go there, learning from childhood the futility of wishing for things to be different.

CHAPTER 5

*T*he next two days went by in a blur. She replied to the message, deleting and retyping her response several times before finally pressing send. She'd written long replies, she'd written enquiring ones, she'd responded looking for more information, and she even wrote one saying she would have no interest in meeting him, but they were all deleted before she sent them. Finally she settled on her reply.

I'll be there. Looking forward to meeting you. Carmel

Bill had gone off to the mart in Nenagh, so he'd be gone all day. The gods were smiling on her, she thought. In a rare stroke of luck, Julia too was busy. She had an in-service day, so she was away at the education centre in Cork attending some conference. Julia dropped the NAPD into her conversation as often as she could, discussing the importance of the National Association of Principals and Deputy Principals as if it were the G8. That was track eight of Julia's Greatest Hits.

She glanced at the clock again. It was noon now and the bus was at 12:35. It would arrive to Dublin at 1:40, and if she jumped in a taxi, she would be at the Gresham on O'Connell Street by two.

She scribbled a note. *Gone out for the day. Not sure what time I'll be back. Carmel*

The journey to the bus stop was uneventful, timing it as she did to arrive with only minutes to spare. Linda McGrath acknowledged her as she stood waiting but mercifully didn't stop to chat as she was dragging her cavoodle, Misty, behind her. That dog hated walking, and Linda was Ballyshanley's premier power walker, complete with peach Lycra tracksuit. Misty refused to budge, lying flat out in the middle of the road, the poor animal probably praying it got hit by a car to put an end to its miserable existence of having to trek 15,000 brisk steps a day. Carmel stifled a smile.

Waiting were two German tourists carrying backpacks bigger than themselves and a pair of teenagers who were too busy snogging the faces off each other to notice her. Imagine, she mused, a pair of sixteen-year-olds with more experience of intimacy than she had.

The bus pulled into the square, and she stepped on board and bought a ticket, trying not to look conspicuous. Why shouldn't she go to Dublin? It was a perfectly reasonable thing to do; women from Ballyshanley did it all the time. She overheard them around the town, the 'yummy mummies', as Julia called them, young women with huge cars and baby paraphernalia that looked like it could be used to attempt a lunar landing. They'd meet in the local organic café, Raw, for chai lattes, wearing their designer clothes with their designer babies, and say how they were just nipping to BT's to pick up something for a wedding. BT's was Brown Thomas, a very expensive shop on Grafton Street. Carmel had never set foot inside the door. On the very few occasions she was in the capital city, she ran quickly to Penney's to pick up a few bits and pieces, underwear or a pair of shoes for cheap.

The bus left her off on the quays, and as she stepped onto the Dublin streets, she felt at home. Trinity House was right in the heart of the city, and sometimes Sister Margaret would take them on walks around, showing them the various places to do with Irish history. A bit of a closet republican was Sister Margaret. Carmel and Kit used to giggle as the nun would recite the Irish Proclamation of independence outside the GPO, reminding the children that the Irish State was founded there on Easter Monday 1916 on the premise that Ireland would cherish all the children of the nation equally. It wasn't the case, of course. Some kids got fancy houses and nice clothes and parents, while kids like her and Kit and the others got residential care. But it was a nice idea, she always thought.

The crowds milled about O'Connell Street, the huge statue of the Liberator, Daniel O'Connell, dominating. She saw again the bullet holes in the bronze angels that formed the four corners of the monument, bullets fired on that fateful week that determined the fate of a small nation, subjugated for so long. It meant little to her as poor old Sister Margaret was going on about it, but now it felt somehow important. Against all the odds, a group of men and women stood up to oppression and won.

Now Dublin was almost unrecognisable to her, let alone to the revolutionaries of over a century ago. Faces from all over the world, every colour of humanity, every language, seemed to be vying for supremacy on the streets of Ireland's capital. A Dublin accent was just one of many in the cacophony of civilisation that assaulted her senses as she made her way up the wide street.

The Gresham Hotel was another place she'd never been inside. It was as if there were two Dublins – the Dublin of Penney's and discount shops, social welfare offices, flats and institutions like Trinity House, and the other Dublin, the one of BT's and the Abbey Theatre and the Gresham Hotel – and the inhabitants of one didn't cross over into the other. She steeled herself to cross the imaginary barricade from her Dublin to the one of privilege, half expecting the beautifully dressed doorman to stop her and demand to know what exactly she thought she was doing. But he didn't bat an eyelid.

Once inside, she wondered what she should do. There seemed to be people sitting on a variety of fancy sofas and armchairs in the reception area, so perhaps that was where he meant. She chose a small chair facing the front door and sat down, instantly panicking. Should she have ordered something? Was she allowed just to sit there if she wasn't a customer? She tried to steady her breathing. Several people seemed to be just sitting, without drinks or food or anything. Maybe it was all right.

She sat back in the seat, then sat forward, trying not to pull at her dark-green V-necked jumper that she now realised was too tight across the bust. It looked fine, nice even, when she was standing up in her black jeans and ankle boots, but sitting down, she felt like the Michelin Man, her spare tyre bulging over her waistband. She should have had her hair done, but if she'd wandered nonchalantly into Clipz in Ballyshanley this morning for a blow dry, Julia would be sure to hear of it, so she didn't risk it. She'd tried to straighten it herself with a brush and the blow-dryer, but it ended up a bit wonky. At least she had managed to put the boxed dye in her hair to cover her blond roots, and it looked fairly even. Julia said natural blond hair was a bit trashy and brown was a better colour, more low-key. Even though she'd been dyeing her hair brown for years, she still started when she looked in the mirror sometimes.

She'd put on a little make-up but felt uncomfortable since she so rarely wore any. She never had any occasion to get 'glammed up', as they said in the magazines. She knew her eyes – dark blue – were nice. Kit always said Carmel's mother must have been beautiful.

What would Kit make of this? Carmel felt the familiar pang of loneliness.

Kit was killed in a car accident in Australia only a month after she got there. She'd been determined to have an adventure and make something of herself. She was so brave. She'd wanted Carmel to go with her, to take a job in Dunnes Stores and save up enough for the fare and just take off, so they could chance their luck and be someone, not a pair of orphans but young women with their whole futures ahead of them. But Carmel had been too scared, too institutionalised to follow her friend. She regretted that now. Maybe Kit would never have been in that taxi if Carmel had been with her.

They had written religiously every few days telling each other everything. Carmel remembered reading bits of her letters to the nuns in the evenings, heavily censored of course, and their genuine distress when they got the word from the Department of Foreign Affairs that

Kit was dead. Carmel had been inconsolable, especially because the last letter she'd sent to her friend was full of hurt and anger. Kit had written to say Carmel was mad to marry Bill, that she could do better than him, and Carmel reacted badly. Kit had been right, of course – not that she could have done better probably, but that she should never have married Bill Sheehan.

She dismissed the sad thoughts; they were not serving her well when she was jittery anyway.

A waitress appeared at her elbow, 'Can I get you anything from the bar, madam?' she asked, though Carmel thought she detected a hint of bored impatience.

Carmel panicked. 'A…a cup of tea – pot – I mean a pot of tea, but for one person, please, just one pot, one cup…' She flushed, knowing she sounded like an idiot.

'Certainly, madam, and would you like anything else?' the young woman persisted with a sigh.

Carmel swallowed. 'No, no thank you.' She wondered what else the woman might mean. Dinner? A sandwich? An alcoholic drink?

She looked around and realised that nobody else was drinking tea in the lobby, though some men had just been served beer, and she felt a bit foolish. Tea must have been the wrong thing to ask for. The waitress looked none too pleased at having to carry it out, and she mindlessly laid the teapot down, spilling some liquid on the marble-topped coffee table beside Carmel. The table was at a stupid height, level with her knees, so there was no way to drink the tea without looking ridiculous. She picked up the little pot, but tea spilled out of the lid all over the table, some dripping off the table and onto her knees. She didn't even want the stupid tea and now she looked so gauche and foolish. She wished she hadn't arrived before this Sharif Khan; her nerves were threatening to get the better of her.

She tried to steady her breathing. Emotions were just like the weather; they came and went. She tried to practice what she'd learned in an online meditation course, to identify the emotion but not spiral down into it, to be curious about it. Why did she feel like this? *Because I'm freaking out*, she yelled silently at her inner Buddha. It was no good. Attempting calm was all well and fine when lying in bed, but here, as she was about to meet someone who might change her life forever, or who might not turn up at all or worse, appear and show himself to be a total chancer, it did nothing to steady her rapidly beating heart. She hated that she was getting her hopes up. If her life to date had taught her anything, it was that it was the height of stupidity to hope for a miracle. And even if this woman he mentioned was her birth mother, what difference could it make now? She was dead. The message said the woman had spent a lifetime looking for Carmel, but that was hard to believe. Carmel had been exactly where her mother left her all those years ago, and if she had gone there, one of the staff would have told her where Carmel went. She was hardly the Irish Scarlet Pimpernel.

Dolly Mullane, she thought, rolling the name around in her head. She'd even said it aloud a few times to see how it sounded. Was her mother called Dolly? She tried to picture a Dolly, with lots of make-up and fancy clothes, a 'good-time girl' as they might have said long ago. No wonder she got pregnant. She horrified herself with the unkind thought, the very sort of judgment she disliked in others. She sounded like Julia. She would never normally think like that, but maybe she was trying to protect herself by villainising the woman who abandoned her. Carmel hadn't allowed herself to dwell on her birth mother for years. In the home it was a source of regular speculation with the others, the children inventing such amazing people to be their real parents; they were always famous sportspeople, or actresses or singers. But she never bothered with that. One day, when she was about twelve, she was baking with Sister Margaret in the kitchen when someone came on the radio, one of those talk shows, looking to meet their child given up for adoption years earlier. The nun snapped it off immediately.

'No good ever comes of that kind of thing. You're a sensible girl not to be dwelling on it.'

Carmel had nodded. She was a sensible girl. And she would never in a million years admit that she would have loved parents of her own. It wasn't to be. She was told her story once when she asked Sister

Kevin. The news was delivered not unkindly but with an air of finality to it. There were no rock stars or famous people, just a story of an unwanted baby girl who was given up into the care of the state as an infant. Her mother had not been married, and as a result she had taken the only option, to hand her child up for adoption. Her mother was never heard from again, and she left no details, no forwarding address. Despite several couples coming to Trinity House looking for children to care for, an opportunity for Carmel to be adopted never presented itself. She assumed it was because she wasn't pretty enough. She'd seen other children be adopted, usually as babies, people really only wanted the tiny ones anyway. And the pretty ones went first. She was alright looking as a child, not horrible or anything, but just kind of nondescript, so she was never adopted. That was as much as she knew.

CHAPTER 6

'*M*rs Sheehan?'

Carmel started as the man touched her shoulder, interrupting her daydream.

'Ye-yes, that is she – me. That is me. I mean, I'm Carmel,' she finished weakly.

'Sharif Khan.' The tall dark-skinned man stretched out his hand to shake hers. He looked imposing, even more so than in the picture on his website.

'May I?' he asked, indicating the sofa opposite her, placing a leather briefcase on the seat beside him. He sat down elegantly, looking perfectly at ease. He was wearing a biscuit-coloured jacket with a dark-maroon shirt and black trousers, and what surely must have been handmade shoes that were slip-on and tan-coloured, in a sort of soft leather that shone. They didn't look like shoes any Irish man would wear. On anyone else they would have looked a bit femi-nine – she certainly couldn't picture the outfit on Bill – but on this man, they looked incredible.

'Yes…yes of course.' She was tongue-tied. He was so striking. She wasn't the only one to notice either. Several women's eyes were on him, she noticed as she glanced around the lobby. He had short silver hair, and a shadow of silver stubble covered his chiselled jaw. He had burned caramel skin, and that alone made him noteworthy in mostly white Dublin, but it was his eyes that mesmerised her. They were perfectly almond shaped and the darkest colour she'd ever seen anyone's eyes, with long thick lashes. He looked like he was wearing eyeliner, though she knew he wasn't. He smiled at her, revealing even white teeth, yet he said nothing.

Carmel felt uncomfortable under his gaze. He was the most striking and glamorous man she'd ever seen. She shifted awkwardly on the stupid seat, wishing the coffee table was high enough to hide behind.

'I am sorry for staring, but it is quite remarkable. You look just like your mother. For a moment, it was as if she had returned. I am quite taken aback, forgive me.' His voice was deep and he almost purred, and his accent was British and very cultured, like someone out of *Downton Abbey*, but with the tiniest hint of something foreign as well.

He clearly didn't do small talk, no chat about the weather, not endlessly dodging around the issue as Irish people would do. Carmel realised he was the first foreigner she'd ever spoken to properly. There was the Polish girl in the shop in Ballyshanley of course, but that was just 'good morning' or 'thank you', and there once was a missionary nun who came from Ghana to visit Trinity House a few times, but she was Irish.

'It's nice to meet you, Mr Khan...Doctor – I'm sorry, Doctor Khan...' she began, trying to sound normal.

'Sharif, please. May I call you Carmel?' That smile again.

'Of course, yes.' She swallowed. Her heart was thumping in her chest; she was sure he could hear it. She was definitely nervous about what he might tell her, but there was something else. There was something very unsettling about him.

'Now I must ask you, do you know your birthday?'

'The 21st of August, 1976,' Carmel answered. 'I was born in the Rotunda. I have my birth certificate, but there are no parents listed.

My mother's name is given as Mary Murphy and her occupation listed as housemaid, but the nun at Trinity House, where I was raised, told me that a lot of girls who had babies out of wedlock were told to write that name on the paper, probably the most common name in Ireland, and my father was unknown.'

He nodded and smiled. 'Her name wasn't Mary Murphy, and she most certainly wasn't a housemaid. But you *are* her daughter, of that there can be no doubt whatsoever. Tell me, do you have a birthmark on the inside of your right ankle? Dolly mentioned you had a brown spot.'

Carmel tried to steady her breathing. She reached down and opened the zip on her boot, pulling her sock down to show him. There it was, a brown birthmark the size of a penny.

'As I suspected. We have much to discuss.'

He reached into his briefcase and took out a big padded envelope. He held the envelope in both hands and smiled down at it, nodding slowly. 'I have waited for a long time to deliver these to you, Carmel, and I feared it would never happen. I wish Dolly were here, I really do. She tried so hard to find you.'

He handed the envelope to her. It contained something bulky. 'There are thirty-eight letters in there, one for each of your birthdays, and several photographs. There is also a box containing a piece of jewellery. It was precious to her and she wanted you to have it. And some photographs. Your mother made me learn who each person in each photo is so I could tell you, if I ever got the opportunity.'

'Can I get you something, sir?' The same waitress had approached, looking the picture of sweetness and light this time. Carmel got the distinct impression she was much more enamoured with her dazzing companion that she'd been with her earlier.

'Ah, a cup of tea like my friend here would be very nice, thank you.' He smiled quickly and the girl beamed.

'Certainly, sir, just a moment.' And off she tripped.

Carmel's hands were shaking; she couldn't open the envelope. 'I…I don't understand. You say she looked for me but I was where she left me, all those years. I wasn't hard to find.'

Sharif reached over and took the envelope, placing it on the table, then held her trembling hands. 'She tried so hard, I swear to you, I witnessed it, so did my parents, but that's another story, but she was stonewalled everywhere she went. She used to say that it felt like more than just bureaucracy, that it felt like someone didn't want her to find you.'

Carmel's mind raced. If this was true, then why did the nuns say her mother had never tried to contact her? Was it true that she wasn't just dumped on the state, never given a second thought? Surely the nuns would not have deliberately allowed her to believe that she was rejected if her mother was truly searching for her? They were not cruel, and they would have wanted to see her reunited with her mother wouldn't they? They told her the truth. That was her story, that was who she was, and now this man has turned up out of the blue telling a very different tale. Should she believe him? She didn't know him from Adam; he could be anyone.

Maybe it would be better if she never opened the envelope. Her life was what it was – she had a roof over her head, food to eat – what good could any of this do now? Thoughts raced round her mind; a myriad of feelings threatened to overwhelm her. Regret, fear, curiosity, resentment, anger, all vied with each other for supremacy to bubble to the surface. Suddenly she couldn't stay there, in that public place with the whole of Dublin watching on, and this man…she had to get away.

She stood up, not caring if she looked rude or ridiculous. 'I'm sorry. I need to go. I can't…I'm sorry.' She picked the envelope up and held it to her chest and grabbed her jacket in the other hand, almost stumbling in her haste to escape.

Sharif put out his hand to steady her. 'Carmel, please wait.' He placed his hand on her arm. 'This is overwhelming, I understand. Please, take the key to my room – it is on the third floor, 353. I will be busy for the afternoon. I have to meet a colleague at the Mater Hospital, so you may use it in privacy to read your letters.'

Carmel looked at him, then down at his brown hand on her arm. Suspicion and panic were all she felt.

'I can't imagine what this must be like,' he went on. 'I know you must have all kinds of misgivings, I don't blame you, this is a most unusual situation, I accept that, but please, I'm begging you to trust me. I swear mean you no harm.'

'I just can't...I'm sorry,' she said again, barely coherent. She felt her throat constrict and sweat bead on her forehead. She felt nauseous and the room was out of focus now. She sat back down, fearing she would fall.

'Breathe, Carmel, deep breaths...' he said quietly, his face close to her ear. . 'In through the nose, out through the mouth.'

She tried, but her breathing was shallow and panicked. She used to have panic attacks, that was what brought her to meditition, and she's managed to get them under control, but all that work had gone out the window now.

He was close to her, speaking softly so only she could hear. 'Slowly, empty your mind, just focus on your breath. Breathe in cool clear air, expel the feelings of fear.'

She looked at him, her eyes fixed on his. She felt trapped.

'Breathe,' he said again. 'Breathe in blue, breathe out red.'

Slowly her breath returned to normal as she followed his instruction, her eyes never leaving his.

Once she was calm again, he handed her the room key once more and smiled. 'Take your time. My mobile number is written on the envelope. You can call me or send a text whenever you want to talk. If you are hungry or need anything, have room service deliver it.' He reached down to pick up her handbag and placed it over her shoulder.

'It is going to be fine. Dolly loved you so much, and to all who knew her, you were a real person – she talked about you all the time. It must seem strange, of course. I feel like I know you, and yet you have never heard of any of us, but it is all good, I promise you. Read your letters and you'll see.'

Carmel had so many questions but this was not the time. She nodded and took the key. She couldn't even start thinking about what it must look like to take a hotel room key from a man she had only just met in the lobby of the Gresham while her husband discussed the price of yearlings and bull calves with other farmers, oblivious to it all. She didn't care. She wanted to read these letters, in peace, by herself, and maybe fill in the parts that had been missing all her life. Parts she never even really realised were not there.

CHAPTER 7

*C*armel walked quickly towards the lift, feeling that everyone was watching her. Of course they weren't. *People only care about their own lives*, she told herself. In the marble and mirrored interior of the lift, she looked at the handwriting on the envelope again. 'To Whom It May Concern' was written in slightly shaky copperplate cursive. It looked vulnerable, though, as if the writer were trying to sound official, not her real self. Did her mother write this? On the back was Sharif's number, in a different hand – confident spiky black numbers.

She inserted the credit card–style key in the slot of room number 353 – she'd seen someone do that on TV – and to her relief the lock clicked and the little light went green. She pushed the door and walked in. It looked just like any hotel room, she supposed. She'd never actually been in a hotel room before, but in films this was what they looked like. There was an unopened small black hard-plastic suitcase on wheels standing in the corner of the room, but other than that there was no evidence of Sharif Kahn or anyone else. The room was immaculate, decorated in muted shades of cream, terracotta and red, and Carmel thought it was beautiful.

She sat at the little dining area beside the window that had two upholstered tub seats either side, perfectly coordinated with the décor, and placed the envelope on the table. Outside on the busy thoroughfare of O'Connell Street, traffic and people went about their business, having no idea that something momentous was happening in room 353. She took a deep breath, trying to imagine what Dr Dyer would advise at this exact moment.

'Breathe, be still, understand that everything is as it should be, everything happens at exactly the right time.' She could hear his voice stilling her fluttering emotions. Sharif reminded her of Dr Dyer, she realised. He was calm and warm and had a lovely deep voice as well.

She peeled open the seal and put her hand inside. Extracting each item slowly, she placed them on the table. There was a bundle of letters in envelopes, tied up with a gold ribbon, all addressed to Carmel. No surname or anything else, just her first name. The 'C' was a flourish, the rest of the letters smaller. The writing seemed more sure than on the envelope, but it was the same hand for sure. There was also one of those little photo albums, the kind that only fits a few 6x4-inch prints, with a wood-effect plastic cover, and finally a small marble jewellery box. The box was not like any she'd seen before; it was heavy and encrusted with coloured stones.

What to look at first? She fumbled with the ribbon on the letters, eventually freeing them. She opened the first one, extracting the single sheet of Basildon Bond unlined blue paper.

My dear daughter Carmel,

Happy birthday to you, my darling daughter. It is 2013 and you are now thirty-eight years old. I can't believe I haven't seen you for thirty-eight years. I've written to you every year on your birthday, and it is my dearest wish that someday you will read my letters. Writing them makes me feel a little closer to you. I used to write you so many letters in the early days, letters full of regrets and tears and pain, but I'll never send you those. I hope you are happy and loved, wherever you are. I'm sixty years old, twenty-three years older than you, but I have cancer so I don't know if I'll see your birthday next year. It's my own fault – the cigarettes did for me in the end. Cursed things, but I love them. I hope you don't smoke, my love. Lung cancer is a horrible way to go I hear, but Sharif will take good care of me. I'll never stop looking for you, not while I have breath in my body, and even if I fail or run out of time, Sharif is determined to succeed on my behalf. If you are reading this, you'll have met him. He is such a special man, my love – trust him.

With all my love today and every day,

Your loving mum, Dolly

It wasn't until Carmel saw the tear drop on the page in front of her, smudging the ink, that she realised she was crying. Her mother loved her, she really loved her, and regretted giving her up. Nobody had ever said those words to Carmel before. Some of the nuns had been fond of her, she knew that, but to hear someone say that they loved her after all these years was overwhelming. One by one, she read all of the letters. She managed to build up a story of what had happened to her mother. It wasn't anything she hadn't heard a hundred times before, but when it was her own story, the story of how she got to be in the world, it was fascinating. Some letters were short, the pain of loss palpable through the decades; others were long and newsy, as if catching up with an old friend.

Dolly said she had to give Carmel up. She was young and unmarried and was forced into a Magdalene laundry, a workhouse for women who found themselves pregnant out of wedlock. She wasn't given a choice in the matter. She was forced to leave once Carmel was ten days old. Her plan had been to go to England, make some money and come back for Carmel once she was set up, but when she came back to the laundry where she gave birth, they said the child had been adopted. She'd never consented to that, and she railed and begged and tried to fight it, but it was no good. They slammed the door in her face.

Carmel had to stop reading then, panic setting in again. She'd assumed she came out of a Magdalene laundry, but she had no memory of it. All she knew was Trinity House.

Dolly never married or had any more children. She lived and worked quietly in England, in a variety of dress shops and ladies' tailors. She loved clothes. She eventually earned enough to buy a small house in the village of Barton-le-Clay. She had a little business, dressmaking, and she loved it.

Every single year, sometimes twice or three times, as often as funds permitted, she would come to Ireland, looking for her daughter, but she was never given any information apart from the fact that her child had been adopted and there was no way to know anything further. The records were unavailable, she was told. There were new staff at the Magdalene laundry, and nobody remembered her. She wrote of one time, when Carmel would have been five or six, when she turned up at that place again and a nun did see her. The nun told her that her baby was better off, that it was serving nobody well to keep up this silly hunt for a child who was lost to her every bit as much as if the child had died.

That was a hard one to recover from, my love. I didn't want to believe there was no hope, you see. But that nun, she wasn't trying to be cruel. In her own twisted way, she probably thought she was doing us both a favour. Nadia really saved me in the months after that visit. She even took me to Pakistan to visit her family.

The last few letters told of her sadness at selling her little cottage and moving into Aashna House, the nursing home run by the son of her friend Nadia. Carmel learned how close to the Khan family her mother became, and when the time came when she could no longer take care of herself, the welcoming embrace of Aashna House run by Sharif was the obvious choice. Carmel tried to remember if she'd ever met a Pakistani person before Sharif Khan, but she was sure she hadn't.

When she finished reading, she held the letters up to her face. Maybe she imagined it, but she thought she could smell a sweet scent, lavender maybe. Just to hold in her hands letters written to her from her own mother was astounding.

Her eye rested on the photo album; she was reticent, not wanting to shatter the illusion that she'd built up in her head of her mother. As she'd read the letters, she'd imagined Dolly as small, slim and kind-faced, with white coiffed hair and a smart skirt and jacket.

She put the letters down and opened the album. The first photo was in black and white and of a fair-haired baby wrapped in a shawl of some kind. She flipped the photo page and read on the back: *Carmel, five days old, August 1976*

Carmel flicked it back again and stared at the child in the photo. It was her. Carmel as a baby. She'd never pictured herself as a baby before. The nuns had no pictures; there was never a reason to take any.

The next photo was of a couple walking on a beach. The man was long-haired and bearded, wearing a kind of loose flowing shirt and jeans. The woman – or girl really, as she couldn't have been more than twenty– had long blond hair, hanging loose down her back, and a yellow and mustard patterned maxi dress. Both were laughing happily into the camera.

Carmel flipped it over. *Me and Joe, Dollymount, 1973*

So that was Dolly. She was pretty and slender. Carmel tried to see a likeness to her own in the face. She looked at the man more closely. He had fair hair and a kind of straggly beard. He looked like a hippie, but he had lovely straight teeth and a kind way about him she thought. Was this Joe her father?

There were only two other pictures. The first was a group shot taken on a pier, the sea behind them. They were laughing and happy, the dark-skinned Indian or Pakistani woman wearing a bright-pink sari, a tall, handsome man, clearly her husband, with one arm around her shoulder, and in front of them a little boy with almond-shaped black eyes, smiling shyly for the camera. She turned it over. *Nadia, Khalid and Sharif, Brighton.*

The last one was a recent photo, based on the fashion. In it there was a large group of people, sitting in a light filled room, twenty or more, and in the middle of them all, a slight, smiling woman in a wheelchair. She was very thin, and her skin had a yellow pallor. She was wearing a bright-turquoise scarf on her head, tied behind pirate style, and was dressed in an elegant white shirt tucked into jeans. She wore long silver earrings, and around her neck was a necklace with a bright blue stone. The only person Carmel recognised in the picture was Sharif; he had a stethoscope around his neck and was smiling brightly at the woman in the wheelchair. Carmel flipped it over. *Me after chemo at my birthday party in Aashna. Sharif said I needed to take this one with him in it so you'll believe him if WHEN he ever finds you.*

Carmel felt a lump in her throat. The 'if' was scribbled out and 'when' was written over it.

The earrings and necklace are yours now, darling. I got them in Karachi, from my friend Nadia when we went to visit her family. I was a mess at that stage, the lowest point in my life, when I thought you were truly lost to me forever, but she and Khalid held me up when I couldn't hold myself up and I love them.

Carmel opened the box. It definitely looked unusual. There, sitting on the blue satin lining, were the earrings and the necklace Dolly wore in the photograph.

Her phone beeped and she jumped.

Customers please note bin collections this weekend will be on Saturday due to bank holiday.

She dismissed the automated text from the council but noticed the time. It was 4 p.m. Bill would be home in two hours, looking for his dinner, and Julia was surely on the way back from Cork now and could call in at any moment. Panic gripped her. Where had the last two hours gone? She had to get back. She couldn't bear to have to answer their questions about where she'd been all day.

She gathered the letters and photo album into the envelope and was just about to place the box in beside them when she stopped. She opened the jewelled box again and took out the earrings and the necklace and slowly put them on. She stood up and looked in the mirror. She looked dreadful, eyes red from crying, mascara smudged all over her face, make-up blotchy, but she didn't see that. She saw the necklace and earrings, once worn by her mother, now on her.

CHAPTER 8

*T*here was a knock on the door. Carmel started in shock. Maybe it was the hotel management, knowing she shouldn't be in there, coming to throw her out.

'Carmel?' She heard her name through the door.

Sharif! She'd have to open it.

'Just a minute!' she called, running to the bathroom to splash her face. She patted her face with tissue, afraid to use the lovely white towels in case she left make-up on them. Looking marginally better, she opened the door and let him in.

He placed his coat, hat and umbrella on the bed, and placed his leather satchel on the floor. Everything about him seemed so polished, he was like something from a fancy menswear catalogue.

'Hello. Thanks for letting me use the room...' she began, anxiously trying to fill in the silence.

'It was my pleasure.' He smiled, and she noticed how his eyes crinkled.

'I was just going...' she said, making for the door.

'Please.' He laid a hand on her arm once more. 'Please let us order some tea, perhaps some refreshments for you. You have not eaten, I assume?'

Carmel was flustered. 'No. No thanks. I've to get back. My husband…and his sister…they will be wondering where I am and –'

'Please,' he repeated. 'I have some things I want to tell you, things about your mother. I would like to talk to you about her.' His measured and serene manner was in direct contrast to Carmel's disquiet. She looked at him and remembered what her mother had written. 'He is a special man – trust him.'

A wave of defiance crashed over her. All her life she'd done as she was told, didn't ask questions, put herself last. But today, this man was here, probably only for a night or two, and he wanted to talk to her about her mother. Bill and his dinner and Julia and her questions would just have to wait.

'OK.' She exhaled, feeling a little stronger. 'I'd like to hear it. I'm sorry, this is a lot to take in. And I'm sorry for running off earlier – I just got overwhelmed.' She allowed herself to be led back to the chair by the table. Once she was seated, he went to the hotel phone.

'Hello, this is Dr Sharif Khan in 353. Could you please send up tea for two, an extra-big pot if you can, as well as a selection of sandwiches? Thank you.'

He sat opposite her, his dark eyes resting on her face, a small smile playing around his lips.

Carmel felt awkward, needing to fill the silence between them. 'So you're from Pakistan and you're a doctor,' she blurted, instantly realising how gauche that sounded. He would think she was just like Julia, a snob who would just about manage to put aside her hatred of everything foreign for a doctor.

'Yes.' He smiled again, nodding. 'I am from Pakistan, well, my parents are more than me to be honest, though I do have lots of relatives there still, and yes I am an oncologist. The home I run in Bedfordshire in England is a care home for those in the last stages of life. Dolly died there, though I had known her for years of course by that stage. She was a wonderful friend to my mother and to me and my father too. We all miss Dolly very much. We were very close.'

He had a way of talking that soothed her. She could imagine him as someone one would want around if they were dying. Gentle, calm, capable.

'So you saw the pictures? Those pieces of jewellery are lovely on you, by the way. She would have been so proud to see her daughter wearing her precious things. Did you read all of the letters?'

He was comfortable asking delicate questions. Carmel felt when he looked at her that he was gazing into her mind. 'I did,' she managed.

'Can you see the resemblance between her and you?' he asked.

Carmel thought about that. 'Well, there's just that one picture of her when she was young, on the beach, much younger than I am now, but I suppose I can, a little bit.'

'Shall I tell you about her?' he asked, his dark eyes never leaving hers.

Carmel's face must have registered her dilemma. She'd buried her curiosity about her mother all her life as a way to save herself from the emotional roller coaster that meeting birth parents inevitably seemed to cause. Part of her longed to know every little thing, but a bigger part was preserving her heart from more pain by rejecting all of this.

Sharif misinterpreted the reason for her hesitation, however. 'I'm sure he'll understand,' he said quietly, sitting still, seemingly aware that any sudden movement on his part would send her scurrying out the door. 'Your husband, I mean. Perhaps you could telephone him so he won't be worried?'

Carmel stifled a laugh and was instantly aware how loud her reaction was, and how inappropriate it must seem. She felt her cheeks redden and rushed to explain. 'Sorry, you must think I'm awful. It's just that he wouldn't – understand, I mean. Or worry either for that matter. He doesn't know where I am, but he won't care except that his dinner won't be on the table.'

Sharif looked perplexed. 'But he *does* know of your circumstances, the fact that you were adopted?'

'I wasn't.' The pain of years of rejection weighed heavily in those two words.

'Not adopted? But I assumed that you were placed into state care and subsequently adopted. That's what your mother thought as well.' Sharif lost a little of his assurance and composure.

'NO. I NEVER WAS,' Carmel said calmly. She'd toughened herself up to her own story over the years so much it didn't touch her emotionally. It was as if she were telling someone else's story. 'I don't have any paperwork to support this but I was told that I was born in a laundry – that's where they put women like my mother, you know, who were pregnant out of wedlock. I don't know how long I was there, as I say, there are no records. I must have been moved to Trinity House at some stage – that's a children's home out in Drumcondra run by the Sisters of Charity. My earliest memories are in that place so I was definitely there by the time I was around three I think, I spent all of my childhood there. Then when I was eighteen, the nuns told me it was time for me to move on, that the state wouldn't pay for my care any more, but I had nowhere to go. Because I'd been there the longest, they took pity on me, I suppose, and allowed me to stay on as a helper. It wasn't really allowed, and I didn't earn anything, but I got room and board in return for taking care of the little ones and things like that. I used to help in the convent as well with some of the older nuns. I liked it actually – they were lovely mostly.'

Carmel knew her story probably sounded like one of those straight to TV films, the ones that were on on a Sunday afternoon, deliberately to manipulate the emotions, but she could honestly say she could speak dispassionately about it. She did wonder very occasionally where she was, before Trinity, who cared for her, was she ever cuddled as a baby? But that was the path to self pity, and besides what good would it do dwelling on it? There would never be an answer to those questions.

CHAPTER 9

Sharif looked at Carmel in admiration. 'I'm amazed at how you can be so calm. I – we always thought you had been adopted.' He paused. 'But please, I'm sorry for interrupting. Please go on.'

Nobody had ever asked her her story before, not Bill, certainly not Julia, but she found this man easy to talk to, so she carried on.

'Well, I suppose I always knew I couldn't stay there forever. The nuns never put pressure on me or anything, but the authorities used to visit and the sisters were in breach of the regulations by keeping me there – and I hated the idea of them getting in trouble, so I had to think about moving on. But I had no proper skills. I was OK at school, but not brilliant or anything, and anyway further education wasn't available for kids in care even if we did show some promise. I suppose we'd cost the state quite enough already or something. Then one day the Reverend Mother got a letter from a widower, asking if there were any young women interested in meeting him and his children, with a view to marriage. I suppose it must sound like a story from the '50s rather than the '90s – the nuns even remarked on how ludicrous a suggestion it was in that day and age – but I said I thought he sounded nice and I'd be happy to meet him.'

If Sharif thought that it was a mad or tragic story, his face gave no indication of it. 'Go on.'

'And so I met Bill one day in Trinity House, and he was quiet but nice – at least I thought he was. He took me out for a cup of tea, told me about his home and the farm and his little twin daughters. His wife, Gretta, had died, you see, and he was in need of a wife. And so after about three or four meetings, he proposed and I said yes. I felt like I was getting a home and a family at long last.'

The silence filled the space between them, interrupted by a knock on the door. Her heart leapt, her nerves jangling.

'That will be the room service.' Sharif got up and walked over to the door, had a brief word with the porter, tipped him and returned bearing a tray laden with tea and sandwiches. 'So shall I pour?'

She smiled and nodded, glad that the interruption had defused the atmosphere created by her revelations. She took a sip of tea and one of the sandwiches he offered. She was ravenous.

'So did you and Bill live happily ever after?' Sharif asked.

Puzzled by the question, she thought for a moment. Nobody had ever asked her that before. Happy wouldn't be how she'd describe it, but it was bearable. 'I think I was grateful that he wanted me, that he was willing to marry someone with no past, no family to claim her, and he is kind, I suppose, in his own way. He doesn't say much, and he's out a lot. And now that the girls are grown up and gone, well, there's not much to do around the house. But he's never cruel or mean. The problem is that he still loves his first wife, and I'm no match for her. I tried to be, to be a good wife and mother, but it never really worked out. To be honest, we never talk. I...I...' – she struggled to find the right words – 'I disappoint him.'

Carmel flushed red, feeling like she'd said too much. Suddenly the room seemed stuffy and she needed to get out. What was she thinking? Sitting in a hotel room telling a stranger her deepest secrets? She must be losing the plot.

Sharif put his hands together and tapped his mouth with his joined index fingers, deep in thought. Carmel noticed the length of his fingers, the perfect cream-coloured crescents on the nails, so different to Bill's calloused hands, his gnarly fingernails.

'I have a proposition,' Sharif said with enthusiasm. 'Let us walk. You telephone your husband to reassure him there is nothing untoward about your tardiness in returning home, and we will get out into the fine Irish sunshine. There is a park, I believe, not far from here. We can walk and talk, and it may not seem so…intense…as it now does.'

'But you've just ordered all of this food…' She pointed at the tray.

He shrugged. 'Let's take a picnic.' He wrapped some sandwiches in a serviette and put them in a small leather satchel he retrieved from the bed. Noting Carmel's reticence, he added, 'Carmel, we have so much to say to each other. So far, I am in shock. Your life is nothing like we imagined. Your mother waited for this day all of her life. How happy she would be to be here with you now, back in Ireland. I want to hear your story, and I want to tell you hers. But sitting here, in a hotel room with a man you have only just met, well, it must seem a little…awkward, especially in light of the revelations you have had to absorb today. So I propose that we walk, we chat and perhaps we can get a takeaway coffee or a drink if you prefer? This is a strange situation.' He waved his hand around the room. 'Not conducive to relaxed conversation. Surroundings are so important. In Aashna House, when a patient has something they would like to discuss with me, we usually schedule a walk in the gardens. It is much more natural, more normal. You're a married woman, and you are alone in a hotel room with a man you've just met. You and I both know the circumstances, and that there is nothing untoward happening, but it is a tense situation. Of course you would not be relaxed.'

The simplicity of the plan made her smile. He struck her as a man who just did things; he didn't overthink them. Unlike her, who overthought absolutely everything. He also was refreshingly honest. She'd never met anyone like him. Perhaps an afternoon wandering around Dublin with him, learning about her mother, wasn't the end of the world. She both longed for and dreaded hearing the story of how it came to be that she spent her life as a child of the state, and this might be her only opportunity. And he was right about the hotel room; beautiful as it was, it made her feel guilty, though she was doing nothing wrong.

The only part of the plan that she was dubious about was ringing Bill to tell him where she was. She had never rung him once in their whole marriage, nor had he ever rung her. Besides, even if she tried to explain, neither Bill nor Julia would ever understand, not in a million years. They thought they knew her background, and while Bill never mentioned it, it was a source of shame as far as he saw it, and Julia did get in the odd poisoned barb. Carmel was beneath them, that much was made very clear. Her birth family or her past was never going to be dinner table chat.

'I'd like that,' she heard herself say. 'I won't ring him. I'll explain when I see him. It would only...complicate things.'

'Very well, Carmel, as you wish.' He stood up and gave her a grin. He slung the satchel over his shoulder and gathered his umbrella, hat and coat from the bed. It was a knee-length camel wool coat, and his hat was one of those you'd see in films about the war – did they call them trilbies? Anyway, she thought he looked the picture of elegance. She judged him to be in his late forties. The way he moved fascinated her. He was supple and lithe, like one of those big cats seen on nature programmes sometimes. Confident, unflappable, self-assured. Everything she was not.

The weak May sunshine bathed O'Connell Street in thin yellow light as they ambled along. They stopped to look in a window of a shop advertising Irish paraphernalia, and she noted Sharif looking at her reflection in the glass. She caught his eye.

He smiled. 'I'm sorry, it must be disconcerting to be scrutinised like this, it's just you look so much like her. Dolly was a unique person, a free spirit, a lover of risks and jokes, and she had a hatred for conventions or rules.'

'Like the rule that says don't give away your baby, you mean?' Carmel shocked herself with the bitterness she heard in her voice. They started walking again.

· · ·

49

'You're angry, and I don't blame you. What actually happened to you and what your mother *thought* happened were two very different things, but this is what you must understand, Carmel – she was not allowed to keep you. She would have loved nothing more, but the father, your father, was a married man, and even though she went to her grave believing that he loved her, he never left his wife. She couldn't go home. Her father was a very strict man, and her mother died when she was young, just eight years old. She explained to me how powerful the system was at that time, it seems hard to imagine now, but the church and the state colluded to police such matters as pregnancy and adoption, things that were none of their concern.

They decided, because she was a girl with no means or man, she couldn't have you. She was a young girl, alone, with no support, and they made a moral judgment on her fitness to be a mother. Sexuality and morality as they defined it, were closely monitored and if people didn't conform to their narrow view of the correct way to live, they very quickly fell foul of the system. I know it must seem audacious, a Pakistani-British man explaining your country to you, and I'm sure none of this is news, I'm not trying to lecture you, just to say to you what I think your mother would have said if she was here. To explain, you know? They insisted Dolly leave you, and it seems there was no fighting those nuns. They had the back-up of the police inexplicably. She told me of girls who ran away from that awful place they were imprisoned, being picked up by the police, though they'd broken no law. So she gave in with such misgivings, she cried and cried. For months after your birth, she couldn't really function on any emotional level. But they were right about one thing – she had nowhere to go and not a penny to her name. Her plan was to allow you to be taken into care, just for a little while, until she got herself sorted out with a job and a home, numbing her pain and earning as much money as she could, working all the hours, and then she would come back for you.'

'So what happened?' Carmel asked, skirting around a bunch of giggling teenage girls.

'By the time she came back to the baby home to get you, a few months later, she had a good job. She and my mother had set up a dressmaking business in London. She had a little flat, security for you and for her, and she felt she could offer you something more than a life of drudgery and poverty.'

'If all this is true, why didn't they just let her come and get me if it was what she wanted?' Carmel willed herself not to cry. She wanted to believe him, but none of it made any sense to her. 'Nobody else wanted me, so it's not like any adoptive parents would have been heartbroken to lose me. I was burden on the state, so surely they would have been glad to be shot of me?'

'I don't know the answer to that, I wish I did. I can't understand why they wouldn't let you go with her. But the truth is, when she went back, they said you had been adopted and that they couldn't give her any details. She was devastated. She'd never given permission for you to be adopted, and she said so, but they didn't seem perturbed by a little trifle like that. It was outrageous but I suppose some of the old respect for the clergy still existed in Dolly at that stage. She lost that over the years I can tell you.'

Carmel marvelled at how life was going on all around them, people meeting friends, running for busses, buying the evening newspaper, while her entire world was imploding. She focussed on Sharif as he went on,

'They were polite if unhelpful at first, I think, but then she kept coming several times a year, so eventually they just threw her out onto the street and refused to engage with her about it at all. By the end they wouldn't even open the door to her. Each time, she returned to England heartbroken, dejected. I remember nights in our living room over the years, my mother comforting her when I was just a boy, as she cried and railed against the system. No matter what they did to her though, she would never give up. Over and over, she went to Ireland, talking to the authorities, priests, the adoption board, anyone that would listen, saying she never gave permission for you to be adopted, but the mother and baby home management, an order of nuns, claimed that she did and that it was all done legally and above board. Eventually she saved up enough money for a lawyer and it went to court, but the judge ruled against Dolly.

'My mother was with her, and for months your mother could neither work nor communicate properly. She stopped eating, refused to go out, seemed to give up on life. She had one goal, that was to find you, and she felt at that stage that she's tried everything, to no avail. My parents, I'm proud to say, through the sheer will of their friendship, helped her to find a way to live again. Not the life she wanted, nothing like it, but a life nonetheless.'

CHAPTER 10

*C*armel tried to absorb what Sharif had said. None of it made any sense based on her understanding of her past, but she knew instinctively he was telling the truth.

Suddenly a thought occurred to Carmel.

'Did she ever marry?'

Sharif smiled sadly. 'She never did. Though she had many admirers, everyone loved Dolly and she could be charming when she chose to be, she never paid them any serious attention. She only had one goal, and that was to find you. She wrote to you frequently and told everyone about you and explained that she would never give up. The authorities here told her that your name had been changed at the time of the adoption, and absolutely refused to tell her what it was, so it was as if you'd vanished into thin air. They told her that her only hope was if you tried to make contact with her when you were an adult. She waited, from the day of your eighteenth birthday, hoping and praying every day for some contact. She wrote to the Irish adoption board, to charities, to support groups, giving her details, in case you ever tried to find her.'

A middle aged woman passed them, linking arms with an older lady, most likely her mother, and Carmel felt that old familiar pang, a sense of loss that she never even acknowledged to herself. They were sharing a joke and Carmel wondered if she'd found her sooner would she and Dolly have laughed like that together?

'I'm sorry, am I talking too much?' Sharif asked.

She smiled, 'No, not at all, it's fascinating, if a bit bewildering. Please, go on.'

They skirted around a busker playing a Leonard Cohen song on a battered old guitar. Carmel was reminded of one of her favourite quotations, from him. 'There's a crack in everything, that's how the light gets in.' The more Sharif talked, the more she felt the wall of indifference she'd built around herself crack.

'Well, from a patient at Aashna, she heard about using the internet to trace people, and so she went off to the local community college and learned how to use a computer, and I helped her to buy a laptop. She searched and searched again, asking everyone, anyone who had been in care, adopted, fostered, if they ever came into contact with you, but to no avail. Social media, of recent years, has been wonderful – she was in so many Facebook groups set up for people trying to reunite.'

They had walked across the city to St Stephen's Green, where the after-work crowd had begun to appear. People pushed babies in strollers, toddlers and children ran to the ducks with bags of stale bread, and Carmel marvelled again at how ordinary everything was when she felt like her world was being turned on its head. Sharif bought two takeaway coffees from a food truck and sat on a bench, offering her a sandwich from his bag.

She accepted one of ham and cheese, thinking about Sister Lucy saying how unladylike it was to be seen eating in public. She was nice, but did they all lie? All of the nuns that raised her? Or were they spun the same story she was? She hoped they were.

'Did you ever try to look for her?' he asked gently as they ate in companionable silence.

'No,' Carmel answered truthfully. 'I suppose I didn't see the point. I was told I was abandoned and I had no reason to doubt their honesty. Not adopted, not fostered, just dumped on the state discarded, like rubbish. I assumed that if she didn't want me then, why on earth would she want me now? I used to fantasise when I was very young, six maybe, that she would come for me, that it had all been some big mix-up, and we would go off and live happily ever after, but I grew out of that.' Carmel's voice cracked.

'Did they ever say why were you not adopted?' Sharif asked gently. 'Do you know?'

'No.' Carmel shook her head. 'Not cute enough, I suppose. If you don't get taken by age two or three, there isn't much hope. People want babies.' She shrugged.

'That could not be why. I've seen your baby picture. You were a beautiful baby, and you are a beautiful woman. There must have been another reason. Why would they tell Dolly you'd been adopted, but then prevent it from happening?'

Carmel blushed to the roots of her hair. Nobody had ever called her beautiful. A nun once said she had good bones, but that was as close to a compliment as she had ever received. 'Well,' she said, praying her voice wouldn't betray her discomfort, 'if there was some ulterior motive, we will never know. I had no paperwork, which was very unusual, even for kids like me. When Bill married me, I needed a birth certificate, and I found out that there was no file in existence. I was – still am, I suppose – a nobody.' Carmel didn't mean for her tone to sound self-pitying; it was just how she saw it. 'They generated one for me, they had to in the end, they couldn't keep looking at me and saying that I didn't exist.'

'You are not a nobody. You shouldn't think of yourself that way. You were loved by your mother, so much. If she were here now, she'd tell you and then ask you what you plan to do with your life. She was always very direct. She regularly asked me the same thing.'

Carmel chuckled. 'I don't really have any plan. Stay in Ballyshanley, I suppose. Bill will probably put up with me. He'd hate the idea of divorce, it's not the done thing in Ballyshanley, much better stay and be miserable.'

Sharif did not return her smile, but he gave her a quizzical look.

'Do you work outside of the home?' he asked, and Carmel struggled to answer. It was embarrassing.

'No, no, I don't. I would like to have a job, but Bill wouldn't like me to work. He'd feel like people might say he couldn't provide for me.'

'And it seems to me what people might say seems to matter a great deal to him. But what if it wasn't up to Bill? What would you like to do? Where would you like to go? What's your dream?' Sharif probed.

CARMEL LOOKED deep into his eyes, maybe it was because he was a doctor, but though he asked direct questions, it didn't feel intrusive.

She sighed. 'I know I must seem pathetic to you, and I probably am, but people like me, we don't really get to have a dream, you know? We're lucky if things work out OK – that's the best-case scenario. Take, for example, my friend Kit. She was in Trinity House as well, grew up there, just like me. She left care and went to Australia, and she begged me to go with her but I was too afraid. She ended up being killed in a car accident.' The memory of her friend still hurt, even after all these years, but it was important for him to understand. 'I don't mean that it was good to be scared, but just that because she was a kid like me, nobody cried for her, except me and one or two of the nuns. To any other girl, who went off following her dreams to Australia, then it would have been different, tragic, people would remember it for years. There is a family in Ballyshanley, their son died on a holiday in Spain, everyone knows about it, and it's a consolation to his family that he was having a great time with his friends up to the end. It's not that Kit didn't matter as much as him, but I suppose a person only matters in as much as the people around you care when you're gone. And people don't care about people like me and Kit. I'm not saying this to make you get out the violins, it's just how it is. I went from being a ward of the state to being Bill's wife. I never even had a proper job, I've never been anywhere, and I don't have any skills. To get chances, to make something of yourself, at least one person has to be on your side, has to believe in you. Nobody ever did that for me.'

Despite her efforts to stop, her eyes brimmed with tears. She tried to pull herself together, but it was as if a dam had opened and nothing she could do would stop the deluge now.

Sharif handed her a chocolate-coloured silk handkerchief from his pocket. She was afraid to use it as it was so beautiful and smelled of a heady spice, but he took it from her hands and wiped her face. Then he put his arm around her shoulder and held her to his chest. She could hear the beat of his heart, and though every fibre of her being told her that sobbing in the arms of this handsome but total stranger in the middle of the park was absurd, a little part of her felt safe. It was a new feeling, that someone was on her side, that she wasn't alone. She's had so few hugs in her life, Kit had hugged her of course, and one of the nuns embraced her as she left Trinity, a peck on the cheek from the twins on her birthday when delivering a scarf, never with Bill, not even once, so apart from her friend and her teacher, she could never remember one. And certainly never with a man. She should withdraw probably, it wasn't right to be hugging a handsome, foreign doctor in the middle of the street, but she never wanted him to let her go.

He moved back a fraction, still holding her, to look into her eyes.

'You always had Dolly on your side. You just didn't know it, Carmel. She loved you. She loved you so much.' His words, repeated over and over, were like a soothing balm to her battered heart.

She fought the urge to break free, to apologise for her outburst, to run frantically to the bus. Instead, he wrapped his arms even more tightly around her and she stayed there on that bench, cuddled up to him, breathing in the smell of him, a citrusy, spicy smell, and soaking up the comfort of his embrace as he rubbed her head and let her weep for her mother, for herself, for the lost little girl, for the bitter teenager and for the bride who felt she deserved no better than a broken-hearted man's hospitality.

CHAPTER 11

*T*he evening chill was settling in, the heat of the sun gone as it set over the Dublin skyline. Everyone was back in coats and scarves again. They'd sat on that bench and talked for two full hours. Oftentimes in the conversation, without meaning to, she caused him to peal with laughter, a lovely throaty sound. He seemed to find her very funny, which both pleased and astounded her. As the shadows lengthened and the park emptied out, Carmel shivered in her thin jacket despite the heat of Sharif sitting beside her, his arm never leaving her shoulder.

'You're cold. No wonder, you've hardly eaten all day. Let's go for dinner, and perhaps a little champagne, to celebrate?' His eyes twinkled as he took off his scarf and wrapped it around her neck. It was cashmere and smelled of him.

She smiled. 'I've never had it.'

'Not even on your wedding day?'

'It wasn't that kind of wedding,' Carmel said with a sad smile.

Sharif stood up and tucked Carmel's arm in his as they left the park. 'So are we on for dinner or do you need to go?'

'I'd love to have dinner with you.' The words were out before she realised that it sounded like she was agreeing to a date. They walked down Grafton Street, the fancy clothes shops were still open and people milled around happily.

'Wonderful. My colleague suggested a place – it's not far. Shall we go there? There are so many stories to tell you, it's hard to know where to begin. Unless there's a place you would prefer?'

She laughed. 'No Sharif, I don't have a favourite Dublin restaurant. I could take you for a wan and wan but I think your tastes might run to something a bit more upmarket.'

'Oh really? You think you know me already do you?' he teased. 'I've no idea what a wan and wan is, but I'm game if you are.'

'It's really a one and one, and it's what Dubs call fish and chips. We got them a very odd time as kids. Wrapped in newspaper, soaked in vinegar. Delicious.'

'I'll tell you what, next time I'll risk your wan and wan,' he made a bad effort at an Irish accent, 'but if I do you have to try a Pakistani style paratha.'

Next time? Was there going to be a next time? She felt a thrill.

'What is that?' she asked.

'It is like angels dancing on your tongue, minced chicken, with spices and egg, wrapped in think pastry and deep fried,' he kissed his fingertips. ''lateef.'

Seeing her confusion he explained, ''lateef means delicious in Urdu.'

They strolled on, chatting easily until he stopped. 'Stay here, one moment, I'll be back.'

She assumed he needed a bathroom break or something as he ducked in the door of Brown Thomas, a shop she'd never been in but had seen advertisements for. Bill's girls frequently told her they got tops or skirts in BT's when she admired them so she knew the prices were outlandish.

He was back a few moments later bearing a large black and while striped bag, the top tied with a ribbon. He handed it to her.

She held it, assuming it was something he'd bought for himself.

'Well, open it.' He grined.

'What? Why?' She was confused.

'Because it's for you?' his brow furrowed.

Uncertainly she opened the bag and saw inside a cerise pink coat. She took it out in astonishment. The tag was still on it and he pulled it off but not before she saw the price. It was eight hundred euro. Surely that was a mistake? Eight hundred Euro for a coat? It was a Max Mara, a brand she's heard the girls drool over. The lining was blood red silk and she felt so self-conscious as he held it out for her to try on.

'I...I can't possibly accept...' she began, feeling her cheeks burn.

'Of course you can, and that colour is amazing on you. And you're cold, so now you won't be.' He pulled the warm wool collar up and tied the belt at her waist.

'But Sharif, it's too much...and I have a coat at home, I just didn't bring it...' she tried to take it off.

'Please Carmel, let me buy you this, from Dolly, as a gift. She loved bright colours, never seen in blacks or greys or navy. She would have chosen that for you, please.'

His dark eyes pleaded with her.

'Well, alright then, if you insist, thank you. It's the best and nicest thing I've ever had.'

'Good, enjoy it.'

He linked her arm once more and on they walked.

'Why did she never marry?' Carmel asked, relieved there seemed to be no awkwardness.

Sharif paused, then spoke. 'She had lots of offers. One time, I remember this man wanted to take her out. She told me often about him. He was a good man, kind, steady, with a good job and a nice house and car. He tried every way he could think of to get her interested, but nothing worked. She told me she wished she could have fallen in love with him – he was perfect on paper – but she couldn't. She had only had one great love in her life, and that didn't work out.'

'Who was it?' Carmel asked, hanging on his every word.

'Your father.' His arm squeezed hers. 'And she could never then consign herself to a marriage of anything less than that, no matter how convenient or suitable the man might be. She told me one day as we were sitting in the garden having tea, my mother, Dolly and I, that she hoped you were in love with someone who was yours to love and that he loved you in return.'

Carmel said nothing; no words were needed.

'Towards the end of her life she had a friend, a man from Dublin I think, who lived not too far from Aashna, but we never met him. Maybe there was something there, I don't know. She never volunteered so I never asked. She was very open in lots of ways, but there was a part of her that was private, never shared.'

THEY ATE AT THE SHELBOURNE, in a secluded corner lit by candlelight. Carmel had never been anywhere as luxurious. She drank champagne and ate crab and steak that Sharif ordered, he seemed to sense how the large leather bound menu had intimidated her, and they talked as if they had known each other for years. Once or twice Julia and Bill crossed her mind, but she dismissed them. They wouldn't be worried; they would just resent that she had the audacity to go off without clearing it with them first.

She told Sharif stories about Trinity House. She had never considered herself funny before, but Sharif wiped his eyes with mirth at her tales of the nuns and their idiosyncrasies. Like how Sister Josephine was addicted to building programmes on TV and was always telling people where they should put two-by-fours and lintels and RSJs, though the chance of *her* actually doing any construction was zero. Or Sister Finbarr, who couldn't abide Sister Clare, so she deliberately made her porridge with sour milk at least four times a month. As Sister Clare would retch, Finbarr would apologise profusely but would drop Carmel a sly little wink. Or how Sister Margaret had a bit of a crush on Father Lennon and was like a giddy schoolgirl when he came in for his scone and tea after ten o'clock Mass in the church next door. By the time she told him about Julia's Greatest Hits, he was laughing so hard that people were starting to look in their direction.

'Oh, Carmel.' Sharif wiped his eyes yet again. 'You are, as your mother was fond of saying, an out-and-out scream. You have just her sense of humour. She made all the residents and staff at Aashna House laugh every day. They would have the same experiences as she did, but she had a unique ability to see the funny side of everything, and especially of herself. You're just like her. Something about the way you tell a story, it's a gift she passed on to you. She was one of a kind, or at least I believed so until today.'

'I wish she'd found me,' Carmel said quietly. 'Maybe I'd have a great life in England now, making clothes just like my mother. I have a knack for it too, you know? I used to do a lot of alterations for the kids in Trinity House as I got older. I loved the idea of doing it professionally – nothing big, just running up curtains, that sort of thing, maybe even have a little shop. Happy as Larry, with my own money and a little flat and a car.' She sighed wistfully.

'Is that your dream?' he asked quietly. 'An independent life?'

'Maybe,' she conceded. 'It's hard to explain, but it must be nice not to feel beholden, to feel like you've a debt to pay, that you're only being endured because it's the right thing to do or something. I don't know. I probably sound like a right hopeless case.'

'You sound like nothing of the kind,' he said, his dark eyes locked with hers. 'You're a special person, Carmel, just as Dolly was.'

Normally if someone complimented her like that – well, nobody ever did, but if they tried to – she would have batted it away, embarrassed, but she didn't with him. She took his approval with an open heart. Then something occurred to her. 'How did you find me in the end?' she asked.

'Did I not tell you? I am in a Facebook group, it's for people interested in meditation, yoga, nutrition, spirituality, that sort of thing, and so I regularly "like" people on that page, or their posts and so on. There are lots of alternative therapists on there, spiritual people, things I'm interested in. Well, you must have posted something or liked something I liked, so you came up as a friend suggestion. You know the way they do? And I went into your profile, saw your birthday was the 21st of August. I knew Dolly always celebrated your birthday and that she called you Carmel and that she had you in Ireland, so while it was a long shot, it was the best lead we'd had in years. So I did a little digging – Zane, one of the staff at Aashna, calls it Facebook stalking, and he's an expert apparently – and as soon as I saw your picture, I just knew you were the Carmel we were looking for all these years. The rest was easy. Your page is public, so all of your details, your last name, your date of birth and so on, were there to see. From that I set about finding out where you lived. You liked SuperValu in Ballyshanley, County Offaly, and the hairdresser's and a few other businesses in the town. Then using the electoral register online, I found you. Simple!' He grinned. 'Once I was sure you were who I thought you were I sent you that message.'

'Amazing.' Carmel shook her head. 'I don't have many friends around Ballyshanley, so Facebook keeps me sane. Imagine, it led you to me. It's just such a pity that it was too late for Dolly. I know most people think it's only for teenagers, spending all their time on social media. Bill doesn't know what I'm at, and Julia just thinks I'm crazy.'

Did she imagine a hardening of his features at the mention of Bill and Julia?

'I don't think you're crazy at all, quite the opposite. I want to show you something,' Sharif said suddenly, edging his chair close to hers. He pulled his sleek smartphone out of his pocket and tapped a few buttons, then he handed her the phone, resting his arm on the back of her chair. The image on the screen was of a paused video, dated two years earlier.

'What is it?' Carmel asked, realising as she turned her head that his face was only inches from hers. She swallowed, her heart pounding. Perhaps it was the champagne or the rich food, but she knew she had never felt like this before.

'I made this video on Dolly's birthday. My mother threw her a party and invited all the staff and of course the residents of Aashna, some of her and Dolly's loyal customers, a few old neighbours. Everyone, including Dolly, knew it was going to be her last, as the cancer was ravaging her entire system. We were just keeping her comfortable.'

He nodded encouragingly and Carmel pressed play. There Dolly was, her mother, in a wheelchair just like in the photo, the bright scarf round her head as she blew out the candle on her cake.

'Speech, speech!' called several voices in the crowd.

Her mother laughed and looked around. 'All right, all right,' she said. 'I'm dying. D'yez not know that? I'm supposed to be lyin' surrounded by candles!'

The crowd laughed. Carmel was surprised at Dolly's strong Dublin accent. After all the years in England, she'd thought it would be gone or at least diluted, but Dolly sounded like the women who sold the fruit and flowers on Moore Street.

'Seriously, though, thanks to yez all for comin' – 'tis great ta see ye. I won't see most of yez again, in this life anyway, but thanks for every-thin', for makin' me welcome, for bein' me friends. I havta say a special word, though, to me adopted family, the Khans. I honestly don't know how I'da survived without them. Nadia, me best friend, Khalid, her late husband and such a rock of support to me, and their darlin' boy, Sharif. I wanted to dance at your next weddin'. I said I would, but time is runnin' out so I'll havta be there in spirit. Jamilla was a wonderful girl, she wouldn't want you to be alone. Hold on, though, for the right one, d'ya hear me?' She grabbed Sharif's hand and he bent down beside her. Dolly addressed the crowd once more. 'Though he's no spring chicken, he's still a catch!' She grinned as the audience chuckled. She took a sip from a glass, the effort of talking taking it out of her.

'I don't believe in regrets, not really. Ya make your decisions and that's all there is to it, but if there was one thing I'd change, it would be that I'd never have left me beautiful baby girl all those years ago. As yez all know, I've spent years tryin' to find her, but she's out there somewhere, and I hope she's happy and that somewhere deep inside her, she knows that her mother loved her then and still loves her now. So if yez don't mind, I'd like to raise a toast to Carmel, wherever you are, my love.'

'To Carmel,' the crowd echoed.

'A song!' shouted someone.

Dolly laughed, a wheezing laboured sound. 'Well, yez did ask for it, me swan song, I suppose you'd call it…though I'm more like an auld duck croakin' and wheezin'. But I'll give it a go…' Her thin reedy voice struggled to be heard but she persevered. 'When I was just a little girl, I asked my mother what will I be. Will I be handsome? Will I be rich? Here's what she said to me…'

The whole crowd sang along. 'Que sera, sera. Whatever will be, will be. The future's not ours to see. Que sera, sera.'

CHAPTER 12

The video ended and Carmel closed her eyes, placing the phone on the table. Sharif leaned closer and held her hand in his, saying nothing, until the waiter came to clear the table.

'She loved me,' she whispered.

'More than anyone or anything,' Sharif confirmed.

After lingering over coffee, they eventually walked in the direction of the bus station. The last bus was at eleven, so she would make that. They walked in silence, side by side, not touching, through the darkness that enveloped the city, each lost in their own thoughts.

Eventually Carmel asked, 'Are you married?'

He shook his head. 'No. I'm not. I was married once, to a beautiful girl called Jamilla. She got cancer, it was diagnosed too late, and she died. It was then I decided to be an oncologist.' He kept looking right ahead as they walked. 'I never thought I could feel about anyone like I did about her, but I realise I was only a child then. We were so young, twenty-four and twenty-two, a lifetime ago. After she died, I just buried myself in work, and it was enough, it was fine. Aashna House is such a special place. We are a hospice but so much more. We hold retreats, meditations, mindfulness courses, things like that.' He chuckled at the memory. 'Dolly resisted it at first, but in the end she did yoga every day and meditated and the whole lot. By the time she died, she could talk for hours about the nature of consciousness, or what was the soul.'

Carmel stopped walking. 'Wait a minute, are you telling me my mother was interested in spirituality?'

'Yes, it all fascinated her.' Sharif smiled at her incredulous expression. 'She used to listen to guided meditations every day. Deepak Chopra was her favourite.'

'I love him. I have all his books, his CDs, and I listen to his guided meditations all the time too. I just can't believe my own mother was interested in that sort of thing, nobody else I know is. In fact, I've never even met anyone else who was. This day is getting crazier and crazier. I could never have imagined when I woke up this morning that today would turn out like this. It's all been just wonderful. I feel as if my life in Ballyshanley just faded away and this new me has emerged or something.' She smiled. 'Knowing what I know now, I'm going to find it so hard to go back to the old me.'

'Do you have to do that? Go back?' He stopped and turned to her, his features bathed in the glow of an overhead streetlight.

Carmel paused. What was he asking? Of course she had to go back. Her life was there, her husband, her home. *Except they are not yours*, a little voice in her head said. *He's not your husband, not in any way that matters, and that house is not your home.*

Sharif seemed to be thinking, as if weighing up what to say next. Taking a deep breath, he started. 'I am not a rash person. I am naturally very cautious and need to be in possession of all of the facts before I make decisions. I don't know what is happening here, but I know this. I think you are the funniest, sweetest, most beautiful woman I've ever met, and I don't want you to get on a bus to go back to a man who doesn't love you. Please forgive my impertinence. I hardly know you – I'm aware of that – but I have to say what's in my heart. I feel...I don't know...a responsibility or something of that nature towards you, and something else too, and I know your mother would hate to think you were in an unhappy situation. To me, it sounds as if your husband loves a ghost and there is no room for you.'

Blood thundered in Carmel's ears. Nothing ever happened to her, life just plodded along. This was surely too good to be true, but there was a truth to what Sharif said, a fundamental, honest truth, that was impossible to ignore.

'Maybe that's the case, in fact I know it is, ' Carmel conceded, 'but I don't have any options. I've no money, no skills, nowhere to go. Even if I could leave, and I'm not saying I could, I made a commitment. What then?'

Sharif shrugged and smiled.

'You could make a new life, start again someplace new. Have the independence you dream of.'

Carmel laughed sadly. 'Just walk off into the sunset is it? In films or novels maybe that could happen, but this is real life unfortunately, so I have to get back on that bus to Ballyshanley and just get on with my life. It's all right, not awful or anything. I can manage, I always have. '

'Did you not want to have children of your own?' he asked quietly.

Carmel paused. This was raw. She could make something up, say her reproduction system was defective or something, but she didn't want to lie to this man. Something about this night, the integrity of it, the honest way they spoke – it would feel like a betrayal to lie. Excruciatingly embarrassing as the truth was, she would have to tell him.

'I would have loved it, a family of my own, a baby to cuddle. I would have adored it. But...' She coloured.

'But what?' he asked.

'That side of our, em...our marriage...never actually happened,' Carmel mumbled, mortified. 'I wasn't, em...well, Bill didn't want to, and I have no clue, so... Gretta, that's his first wife, she was so pretty and so much better... Maybe he couldn't...I don't know...' Her voice trailed off.

' Are you serious?'

Carmel nodded, her cheeks blazing with shame.

'Bill didn't...look, I just wasn't the right...' she tried to explain.

'The man sounds like a fool,' Sharif said, unusually forcefully.

Carmel smiled and tried to restore the equilibrium of the earlier, more joyful conversation. She didn't want her perfect evening with this incredibly handsome stranger to end on a sad note.

'He loved her so much, and so did the twins, that I think it was just that he can't ever let go. That's not his fault. Honestly, I know it sounds like a desperate sad story altogether, and in some ways it is, but it's all I've ever known and he's not a bad man. I do wish things were different, of course I do, and I tried so hard at the start, but some things are just set in stone, I suppose.'

'Have you ever been in love?' he asked.

It was such an intrusive question, and if anyone else had asked her, she would have recoiled. 'No, never,' she admitted. 'The first time I ever heard anyone say they loved me was today, in those letters from my mother. Kit loved me I think, but we never said it and I doubt anyone else ever did.'

A single tear formed on his dark lashes and travelled uninterrupted down his cheek. 'You deserved so much better than that,' he said, his voice different now, huskier.

Carmel shrugged. 'Not everyone gets the fairy tale, Sharif.'

He stood before her, this exotic man, as the breeze from the River Liffey ruffled her hair. Though she had no experience of anything to do with the opposite sex, she felt something change. His feelings of compassion and benevolent kindness, brought about by his obvious closeness with Dolly were obvious, but there was something else too. Maybe she was imagining it – maybe she'd wake up in Ballyshanley and this would all have been a dream – but there in that moment, something was happening. She was certain of it.

She snuggled into her beautiful new coat, it's luxurious cashmere protecting her from the cool breeze. The darkness had fallen now but the scene was illuminated by the streetlamps along the quayside, the cars and busses that snaked endlessly around the city, and the ships coming in and out of Dublin Port.

Standing before her, he ran his hand through his silver hair, some of his earlier composure absent. He wasn't uncomfortable, but she could see there was an inner turmoil in this man. She barely knew him, but something made her feel like she'd known him for years. His position, his career, his wealth, his accent, all of thise things had intimidated her but not anymore. She saw past all of that and just saw Sharif Khan as a fellow human being, and she longed to quiet his discomfort. He shoved his hands in his pockets and seemed to compose himself to speak.

'Carmel, the only reason I came here to Dublin was because I wanted to do the right thing by my old friend. I made a promise, and I was happy to be able to keep it. I felt so immeasurably sad that it took this long to find you, and that she didn't get to meet you in person, but at least I found you. But now that I've met you, I don't know. Things are different, and I never expected it. I imagined I would meet you, tell you about Dolly, give you the letters and things and get back on the plane. But I find myself in a completely different situation to the one I anticipated.' He sighed.

'Am I imagining this?' he asked.

Carmel didn't need him to clarify what he meant bu 'this', she knew.

She could just shake her head. And he smiled.

'I was in love once, and, well, that's a long story for another day, but Jamilla is gone, she died. She will always have a little place in my heart, but I am here and so are you. I've just met you, and you're married, and none of this makes any sense but we are alive, and we can feel, and I think we both know something is happening here. And who knows where this is going, if anywhere, but I just know I don't want to say goodbye. The thought of you getting on that bus, going back to that man who doesn't appreciate you, hurts me in a way that I can't quite explain.' The calm composure seemed to be gone and he sounded so vulnerable.

Carmel couldn't believe what she was hearing. Was this real? No man she'd ever known was as vocal on the subject of his feelings as Sharif. It was exhilarating and a little disconcerting.

'How about this? Come back to England with me tomorrow. We'll take it from there. You could work at Aashna House – I just know our residents would be overjoyed to meet long-lost-baby Carmel and you'd cheer them up so much, just as your mother did before you.

Your smile, your humour – it's irresistible. You could do that, or maybe start up our mothers' dressmaking business again. There are some little apartments in the grounds where some of the staff or residents who are still able to care for themselves live. You could stay there until you decide what to do next. There would be no pressure Carmel, I'm not asking for anything at all, except perhaps an chance to see what might happen. What do you say?'

His eyes burned with hope and trepidation. Carmel wanted to hug him. It was like a film or a novel, but she never for even one second thought things like this happened to real people, people like her. But yet this gorgeous, funny, kind man, who knew her real mother, was standing in front of her in a Dublin street asking her to leave everything, leave Bill and Julia and all the rest of it, and start again. A new life, one of her very own. She'd be there because she wanted to be, and more importantly because someone else wanted her to be there too. It was terrifying and thrilling simultaneously. She'd never made an emotional decision before; in fact she'd made very few decisions. She was the kind of person who things were decided for. But maybe she could grasp this chance, the chance to be happy, to have her time here on this earth mean something.

He's a special man, my love – trust him. Those words again. It felt as if they were being whispered in her ear. Was her mother guiding her? Or was that fanciful just because the prospect of a new life was so appealing? A wave of icy reality crashed over her. This was insane. She couldn't just up and go, leave her husband and swan off into the sunset with this man. It was crazy. And wrong. She'd made a promise before God, in a church, 'till death us do part'. She couldn't just renege on that promise now, could she?

They were standing outside a busy pub, and judging by the singing coming from inside, there was a party in full swing. Sharif stood before her, not touching, but so close she could almost feel the heat from his body.

Carmel looked up into the face of the man she had met eight and a half hours previously. Nothing about any of her life made sense until this moment. She was always the outsider, someone to be endured because there was nowhere else for her to go. Though it made no sense, with Sharif she felt like she had come home at last.

Home. That word. She'd grown up in a children's home that was nothing like a home in the true sense, and Bill's cold empty farmhouse in Ballyshanley was never really home either. Could she take this offer of a real home of her own?

He's a special man, my love – trust him.

Carmel felt the presence of her mother in a way she couldn't describe and made a decision, the first big one of her life that she'd ever made for herself.

'Are you sure? I mean, you don't have to...just because you promised Dolly...' Carmel wanted to be clear.

'I know I don't have to, as I said, this was never my intention. I want to. I want to have you in my life, Carmel. It seems rushed – I know that. And if you knew me better, you'd realise how out of character this is for me. But something is telling me to hold on to you and never let you go.'

Someone emerged from the pub, talking on his phone. He was a little drunk and swaying slightly, and Sharif moved forward to encircle Carmel with his arms and move her out of his path. Through the open door they could hear the sounds of a raucous party, and the crowd singing...

'Que sera, sera, whatever will be, will be. The future's not ours to see. Que sera, sera.'

CHAPTER 13

*C*armel changed the channel on the small battery-powered transistor to the tinny sound of the news jingle. The incessant chatter of the DJ on the music station was getting on her nerves. Bill was out. The atmosphere between them was still frosty.

That day she got off the bus from Dublin, he had sat silently as Julia harangued and cross-examined her about where she'd been. She'd told them the truth.

'Are you mad?' Julia had demanded. 'You expect us to believe that this black fella claiming to be some kind of a foreign doctor turned up out of the blue and had this fairy story about your misfortunate mother and you swallowed it all? And then, as if running off to Dublin and telling your husband lies weren't enough, you stayed out all night? In a hotel, you say. On your own. And by the way, don't think we don't notice the cheap tawdry baubles you have hanging from your ears and around your neck. Gave you those, did he? Your fancy con man? Well, if you expect us to believe that, you must think we came down in the last shower.'

Julia was so incensed that a globule of spit landed on Carmel's cheek. She wanted to cry, to have them understand, but she was frozen inside.

'We took you in out of an orphanage, a girl with nothing but shame in her background, and this is our thanks?'

Bill always almost winced when Julia mentioned the orphanage, as if he didn't want reminding of his wife's humble beginnings.

'Give me those letters. Get them right now,' Julia demanded. 'Your con man probably wrote them himself.'

'Sharif is not a con man, and no, they're private. They're mine,' she'd managed.

'You are his wife!' Julia hissed, pointing at Bill, who just sat sullenly at the table. 'You cannot have secrets from him. Hand over those letters this minute.'

Carmel shook her head. 'Bill, I promise I'm telling the truth...' She tried to get through to him, but he never looked in her direction.

'Bill, tell her to hand over the letters,' Julia demanded of her brother this time.

'I'm going out,' was all he said, as he stood and pushed the chair back. He strode out of the room and closed the door, leaving Carmel alone with Julia.

'You've been such a disappointment to him,' Julia began. 'It wasn't too much to ask, in return for all you've been given, but you couldn't even be a good wife to that poor man who has provided you with so much more than you deserve.'

'I tried, Julia, I did,' Carmel said sadly.

'Oh ho! You tried, did you? Going off to hotels with strange men, making a show of yourself, and us into the bargain – that's your version of trying to be a good wife, is it? No wonder your mother found herself in the family way. There's bad blood in you, and Bill should never have brought you and your filthy past into this house. If poor Gretta could see what kind of person is in her home now, the poor girl would turn in her grave.'

After delivering that final blow, Julia had mercifully stalked out then in high dudgeon, much to Carmel's relief.

Carmel had gone upstairs after that and moved her things into the spare room. She couldn't sleep beside Bill now. The envelope with the letters and the photographs, as well as the little jewellery box, were hidden carefully, in a place where even Julia's snooping eyes couldn't find them.

That was last week, and ever since, she could settle to nothing. Bill appeared for meals, ate them silently and left again. He made no comment about her moving to the spare room. She tried to keep busy, to stop the endless thoughts going round and round in her mind. The day before, she'd cleared out the hot press, discarding ancient pillow-cases and frayed sheets, and this morning she was determined to give the cupboards in the sitting room a good going over. But nothing could take her mind off what had happened in Dublin.

She could have done it, gone off with Sharif when he asked her, made the new, amazing life he talked about. When he suggested it over that delicious dinner and wine, it all seemed so possible, so entic-ing. But the cold reality of the morning after, as she lay awake, alone in the Gresham Hotel in the room he'd booked for her, was that, of course, she couldn't just up and leave. That was fine on TV shows or in romantic novels, but for ordinary women living ordinary lives, running away with handsome strangers was just not an option, no matter how tempting the offer. It was foolish to think she could. She left Sharif a note, thanking him for such a lovely night, for the photos and letters from her birth mother, for finding her, but explaining she had to go back to Bill.

On the bus back to Ballyshanley, she'd googled Aashna House about fifty times; it looked every bit as beautiful and peaceful as he said it was. She gazed at the picture of Sharif on the staff page, in his suit and white coat, a gentle smile playing around his lips. The pain in her chest was real.

As she washed the breakfast dishes in the sink, the details of their day together, what it felt like to be with him, crowded into her mind. Did she dream it? Did this man really find her on Facebook? Offer her a better life with him, and all the memories of the mother she never knew? And if this magical thing really happened, what on earth was she doing back in the kitchen of Bill Sheehan's farmhouse in County Offaly?

She cursed her cowardice and her sense of duty. She just couldn't do it when push came to shove, as Sister Dympna was fond of saying. The nuns who reared her would have been so disappointed if she had chosen to leave her marriage, to run away with another man to England.

The fact that the stranger was the most attractive man she'd ever seen would surely only compound what would have been already a mortal sin.

No, she thought as she wiped down the countertops for the fifth time, she'd stay no matter how awful it was. To do anything else would be wrong, and on top of it all, she was married in a Catholic church, in the eyes of God, where she promised to love Bill for better or worse. Well, she mused, she didn't know about better – there were few, if any, of those days in all the years – but these were certainly worse days.

Her mind kept returning to her mother and the letters she left with Sharif. The idea that her mother spent a lifetime searching for her to no avail both cheered and saddened her. So her birth mother had not in fact dumped her in an orphanage and forgotten about her.

The precious letters her mother wrote were secreted away where neither Bill nor Julia would ever find them. Bill couldn't care less, she was sure, but Carmel knew Julia regularly let herself in when there was nobody at home for a good poke around, even before all of this, though she had no idea what the other woman was trying to find.

All these new feelings flooded her mind. Sharif had told her that Dolly tried everything to find the baby girl she had been forced to leave in the care of the state but met blank walls of opposition from the Church authorities each time. But yet, she was never adopted. Why? And if she was so wanted, and the authorities knew it, why not just hand her back to her mother? Dolly wanted her, and clearly nobody else did, so why all the secrecy and lies? It was so much to take in.

In the days since the blow-up, she'd made a decision. No matter how much he resisted it, she would have to speak to Bill, alone.

She replayed the impending conversation in her mind once more.

No tears or recriminations, if anything would make him run for the hills it would be crying, no, she would just calmly ask him the question and he would answer her straight. She deserved that much surely? Never once in all these years had she questioned him, asked him why they were here together, living out this charade of a life. Sharif had asked her why and she couldn't answer him. Maybe it was because she thought she didn't deserve any better or something, but she owed it to herself to at least have one proper conversation, even if the thought of it made her nauseous with nerves.

The crunch of tyres on the gravel outside brought her back to reality; Bill was home early for lunch. She swallowed down the panic; she could do this. He'd been visiting his solicitor in town. She only knew that because she'd overheard him on the phone to one of the twins; apparently, he was giving each of them a site on which to build a house. He imagined, in his foolishness, they'd come back and live in Ballyshanley, but Carmel thought they would do no such thing. The girls hated Ballyshanley and its provincial ways; they were city slickers through and through. They would build the huge fancy mansions all right, but as soon as they were ready, the girls would say they couldn't move jobs or whatever and they'd sell the houses and buy even grander places for themselves in Dublin, miles away from County Offaly. Julia had dropped several heavy hints about how a few sites for herself would be ideal as well, but Bill either didn't hear it or chose to ignore it.

Bill, being the only boy of the Sheehan family, got the farm, and his sister got the college education. That was how it was back in the day. But even though Julia drew a fine salary from the Department of Education, had a nice house of her own in the village and would get a big, fat pension when she retired, Julia wanted more. She'd been going on about the price of land rezoned for residential property and how she could do with a nest egg to provide for her in the future.

Carmel never understood it. Julia never went anywhere and had been wearing the same clothes for years. Just greed, she supposed. Julia felt very put out that Bill got the farm in the first place and always acted as if they owned it together. Bill, Carmel knew, felt no such thing. Bill wasn't passionate about anything, but he loved his farm, and it was his, and nobody else's.

CHAPTER 14

The back door opened and in Bill came. Dressed in his good suit, he looked so uncomfortable. He said nothing, gave no greeting, but went straight to his bedroom to change into his working clothes.

When he emerged a few moments later, she thought his face registered a bit of surprise that his lunch wasn't on the table. She snapped off the radio, and the silence in the big old-fashioned kitchen was deafening.

'I'd like to talk to you, Bill,' she heard herself say, her voice sounding strangely formal to her own ears.

'I'm late with the milking –' he began, but she interrupted him.

'I'm sorry, but this is important.' Her voice was stronger than she ever imagined it could be.

'What is it?' He sighed, as if she bored him with emotional demands every day of the week when quite the opposite was the case.

'Why did you marry me?' There. It was out. The question that had plagued her for seventeen years.

'What?' Bill's face wrinkled into confused distaste, and he went to the back of the door for his jacket; clearly he wasn't staying around for this.

Carmel knew she'd never get the guts to do this again, so she ran to the door, barring his exit. 'Please, Bill, I'm not looking for a fight, but I really want to know. Why? You came to Dublin looking for a wife and someone to be a mother to your two daughters, and I agreed, but from that day to this, we've hardly spoken to each other. The girls never wanted me here, and Julia certainly doesn't. We don't have a…' – she felt her face redden – 'normal marriage in any sense. You don't seem to need or want me for anything but cooking and cleaning, and you could have employed someone for that, so I don't understand – why did you marry me?' Her voice was raised now and she felt less in control, but she needed to ask it. She was blushing furiously and could feel her cheeks burning with the shame of it, but she had to plough on. It was now or never.

Bill stood in front of her, his eyes downcast, and it was impossible to know what he was thinking. Long seconds passed.

'Please, Bill, I'm just trying to comprehend what has happened…' She knew she sounded pathetic, but maybe pity for her would make him speak.

He sighed. 'For God's sake, Carmel, I've work to do. I don't have time for this…' He made to pass her.

'No!' she almost shouted. 'I've done everything you asked of me for seventeen years, but we've never had a proper conversation, not once in all that time, and I just don't even know what I'm doing here.'

He looked at her as if she had taken leave of her senses. This was not the Carmel he was used to. He apparently realised there was no getting away from her, so he blurted, 'Right. Fine. Gretta was gone and I thought it would be a good idea. It turns out it wasn't. The girls didn't take to you, and I don't need another wife. I had a good one and she died.'

Each cruel and heartless word fell like a rock on her head. He didn't mean to be horrible; it was just how he saw things.

'I tried with the girls, but Julia…' she began.

'I know, she took over. Look, 'twas either marry someone and have them in here or have Julia, and I didn't want that. She was angling for it from the minute Gretta died, but it's more the land she's after and she can go and whistle for that. This is my farm, not hers, no matter what she may think.'

Carmel heard hard determination in his voice. Being reared with nothing meant this deep feeling Bill and Julia had about land and ownership was lost on her, but Carmel had lived in rural Ireland long enough to know that people would do anything, literally anything, to protect their land.

'So I was brought in just to stop your sister moving in here and taking control of the farm? I was just a pawn to be used?' She tried to keep the raw pain out of her voice; she needed to be as matter-of-fact as Bill was.

'Well, I thought it would work out better. I didn't consider how Julia would turn the girls against you. She was going to resent whoever I brought in, but she was doubly shocked when she found out I'd taken someone out of an institution. I knew you came from a laundry and that you were the child of an unmarried mother, and I thought that might be better than marrying someone with a family of their own and expectations.' He shrugged.

The term 'unmarried mother' jarred with her; it was such a judgemental phrase. She and Dolly were just people who fell afoul of the Irish Church and state in less enlightened times. 'And someone like me would have no right to have any expectations? Because I was worth less than someone born to married parents?' Carmel fixed him with a stare despite trembling inside.

He thought again before he spoke, then delivered each word with painful slowness. 'Well, not that. If I thought like that, I wouldn't have married you. 'Twasn't your fault. You can't be blamed for, well, whatever your mother was. But you're right. It was a mistake. But here we are, and there's nothing either of us can do about it now. I wish it had worked out, for the girls too, but it wasn't to be.'

Carmel tried to ignore the slight against her mother, as if becoming pregnant was some kind of awful sign of her character. 'But if you saw Julia trying to undermine me with the girls, why didn't you say something?'

He shrugged. 'That's women's business, rearing children, girls especially. I just thought you'd work it out.' He shrugged on his working jacket. 'Now I've to go milking.'

Before she had time to react, to say anything, he was gone out the door. She stood in the kitchen, trying not to cry.

She went upstairs, took her letters from inside the insulated lagging jacket on the hot water tank and locked herself in the bathroom. She put the lid down and sat on the toilet. One by one, she reread her mother's letters, taking comfort from them. Somebody loved her. Someone she hadn't seen since she was a baby, someone she couldn't remember, someone who spent her life searching for her daughter.

As she was reading, she heard the back door open once more. Like a thief caught in the act, her heart thumped wildly as she stuffed the letters back into the envelope and shoved it back in the hiding place once more, arranging the sheets and towels carefully in the hot press around the tank. She stood up and examined her tear-stained face in the mirror.

'Carmel? Carmel!' Julia's sharp voice rang out.

Carmel splashed water on her face but knew it wasn't going to help disguise that she'd been crying. She called, 'I'm in the bathroom.'

No response.

Eventually, she left the bathroom.

Julia was on the landing. 'What were you and Bill talking about?' she barked.

'What? Nothing... I...' Carmel knew she must look like a rabbit caught in the headlights.

'Don't lie to me. Bill was parked up outside his solicitor's office this morning, then as I was coming in, he nearly blew me off the road. Has something else happened? What have you done now?'

Carmel hated it when Julia spoke to her as if she were one of the misfortunate kids under her command in the primary school. A loathing she'd never known before welled up inside her. She'd never hated another human being before in her life, but she really hated this hatchet-faced old witch. If Julia hadn't stuck her pointy nose into their business, maybe she and Bill would have been happy, she might have connected with Sinead and Niamh and made a home and a family, but the reason they were all so miserable was Julia.

CHAPTER 15

*C*armel thought in the early days the reason their marriage was such a disaster was because she was so much younger than him, or maybe she just hadn't anything interesting to say, or she wasn't attractive enough, but she was wrong. Bill's admission only confirmed what she always suspected: he never wanted to marry her, or anyone else. Julia had it all worked out that when Gretta died, she'd move in, take over the girls and the running of the house, and when Bill died, she'd get everything. The girls had no interest in the farm, a financial settlement would do them fine, but Julia would finally own the land. Bill's marriage to Carmel ruined all her plans. Bill might have been different, if she'd been able to get through to him, without the wall of Julia between them all the time.

Carmel tried to visualise her mother, imagining her as Sharif described her: brave and impossible to intimidate. She tried to channel Dolly's strength and tenacity. The horrible furry wallpaper on the stairs, the swirly orange and brown carpet, the dark brown painted bannister, none of it was her choice. Nothing in this life or this house was. If she didn't stand up for herself she would be these people's slave forever.

Julia was livid, her dark hair scraped back off her head, her pointy features and rake-thin body almost quivering with temper. 'Tell me what's going on this minute!' she demanded.

'If you have a question for your brother, you should ask him, not me.' Carmel spoke quietly.

'What? Don't you tell me what to do,' Julia sneered. 'He's up to something, and by the way, lady, so are you. I don't believe that fairy story about the Black man above in Dublin for a moment. If something is happening with my family's land, then I have a right to know.' Julia moved closer, her face only inches from Carmel's. Her breath smelled foul.

Sounding much more confident than she felt, Carmel responded. 'No, you don't actually, Julia. This land is not yours, it is Bill's and mine, and one day it will belong to Niamh and Sinead. You don't feature anywhere.' She had no idea where all this strength was coming from, first challenging Bill, and now Julia. It had taken seventeen years, but it felt good. She had hit a nerve with her sister-in-law.

'Yours! You don't own anything!' Julia's cheeks reddened and her eyes flashed with fury at Carmel's audacity. 'You're forgetting something. I know full well who and what you are. A worthless nobody whose dirty slut of a mother went off no doubt with every Tom, Dick or Harry that wanted her, then dumped her child to be a burden on the Irish taxpayer. How dare you place yourself above me.'

Carmel took a step back, to avoid Julia's odious breath. She steeled herself. All the insults, slights and cruel remarks made by her sister-in-law over almost two decades were there, hanging in the ether, but not as a way to hurt her, but as fuel for her rebellion.. Carmel had never in her whole life spoken out – she was a background person – but her mother was not a slut and Carmel was not worthless. She smiled serenely, knowing it would drive Julia mad. When she spoke, her voice was calm and reasonable.

'Why does anyone have to be above or below anyone else? You decide who goes where in your stupid, mad, bigoted head – why? What does that do for you? Does it make you feel superior or something? Because if you need to run others down in order to think well of yourself, then you have a serious problem. And another thing, why does the farm matter so much to you, Julia? You have a fine house and all the money you could want, and yet you drive yourself crazy about this bit of land? Bill won't leave it to you. He'll leave it to me and his daughters – legally he has to – and even if he didn't, he'd rather leave it to the Dog's Home than see you installed here. You constantly sniffing around, looking to see what you can get – dropping hints as subtle as a bag of hammers about sites and all the rest of it, it's pathetic. Do you know that Bill only married me to make sure you didn't move in? He told me so himself, ask him if you want. Why do you think that was, Julia?'

Carmel didn't know where this strength was coming from, but she found herself emboldened by it. 'You turned Niamh and Sinead against me, and they were only little girls. I could have loved them – I wanted to – but you had to drip your poison into them like you always do. The kids in the school are terrified of you too, did you know that? Every single child in Ballyshanley dreads going into third class because you're the teacher, every parent too. The church choir wish you'd just leave them alone, insisting on doing every solo, and they don't speak up because they know how vindictive you can be so they're afraid of drawing your wrath on them. And before you go looking for someone to blame, you've created this for yourself. Your parents provided for you, gave you an education, a house of your own, but it wasn't enough. You could have been happy, but you chose resentment and bitterness instead. What a waste of a life.'

'How dare you!' Julia screamed, slapping Carmel hard across the face.

Carmel was stunned, and her face stung. Julia grabbed her by her shirt and Carmel lurched forward, sending Julia off balance, causing the other woman to lose her footing on the bit of loose carpet at the top of the stairs. She fell backwards down the stairs, landing in an undignified heap below. She managed to get herself up as Carmel froze on the top step.

Once she was upright, Julia spat, 'You will pay for this, you mark my words.' She smoothed down her skirt and tried to fix her hair. 'You should have been left to skivvy for your betters in that place, instead of my brother giving you a respectable home. I know what you were up to in that hotel above in Dublin, even if my brother doesn't. All the time scrolling and downloading whatever filth you'd be looking at on that phone. I know more than you think. You're probably on one of those websites where married men find women – Tinder! Is that it? Is that what you're doing? No wonder you're the way you are. You come from no better,' she hissed.

Carmel placed her hand on the bannister for strength, straightened her shirt and said,

'get out, Julia. Just get out.'

She was suddenly resolute and weary of it all. She walked downstairs, passed the dishevelled Julia and opened the front door. 'Goodbye Julia.'

The other woman had no option but to leave, her thin dark hair escaping the severe bun and her blouse hanging outside of the waistband of her skirt. She glowered as she passed, but said nothing. As Carmel closed the door she heard Julia's car sent up a spray of gravel as she reversed in temper.

Carmel walked into the kitchen. The clock ticked on the dresser; the tea towels she'd used that morning were hanging over the range to dry. Everything looked exactly as it should.

She went to the jar beside the clock on the mantelpiece. In there, Bill kept some cash for the coal man, who was due to call to be paid. One hundred and eighty-eight euro exactly. Feeling a twinge of guilt, she stuffed the money into the pocket of her jeans.

She glanced around, taking it all in before moving to the sitting room. She stood in front of the fireplace and took Bill and Gretta's wedding picture in her hands. 'I'm sorry, Gretta,' she whispered. 'I tried, but there was no room for me. He was only ever yours, and he's all yours again now, not that he ever wasn't.' She replaced the photo and took one more glance around, then slipped her wedding ring off and placed it beside the photo.

She turned to go upstairs. The telephone ringing broke the silence. She thought she should probably answer it, as it was usually someone from the creamery with a message for Bill, but that wasn't her business any more so she let it ring out.

The bed was made; she'd never once in her life not made her bed the moment she got up. She took a pink sports bag, one Niamh used to own, and filled it first with her letters and jewellery box. Then she took her passport, the one she'd applied for thinking she might be asked to go to New York, and placed it in an inside pocket. Then she added whatever clothes she had that weren't too shabby. She didn't have a wash bag because she never went anywhere, but there was one in the main bathroom, probably a discarded one from one of the twins, so she took that and placed her toothbrush and a facecloth in it. She zipped the bag closed and stared at it on the bed. Was that all her life amounted to? A small holdall that belonged to someone else?

She wondered if she should leave a note or something. But saying what? There was nothing left to say.

CHAPTER 16

*A*nother wave of panic washed over her, the thousandth since she'd left Ireland. The overnight journey to England had been OK. She had taken the bus to Dublin and boat from there to Holyhead in Wales as that was the cheapest way to England. She slept a little on the boat; the seats were quite comfortable. But being discharged as a foot passenger at 4 a.m. in a port terminal was grim. There was a delay with the connecting bus, so she'd been cold and tired as she waited with a few other foot passengers. Eventually the coach turned up and the long drive from Wales to London began. They stopped at a petrol station and some people had a cigarette while others got cups of tea, but she didn't want to risk missing the departure so she sat on the coach. She'd never travelled abroad before, so it was terrifying and exhilarating at the same time. Arriving in Liverpool Street station in central London in the mid-morning was something she would never forget.

England's capital was enormous. It felt like they were in the city for ages before the bus pulled into the station, and it seemed like every culture, colour and religion of the world were represented there. She tried not to stare, but everywhere she looked were fascinating sights. A group of men she recognised as Chassidic Jews from a programme on the Discovery Channel on YouTube were walking across the concourse, their long black coats flapping about their ankles. The long ringlets they wore hanging from their temples and their tall black hats made them look slightly comical, she thought, but they seemed to be discussing something of extreme importance. There was a group of Indian women all dressed in the most colourful saris, the vibrant purples and turquoises delighting her. They all talked at the same time and boarded another bus to someplace called Swindon. A man in white wide-legged trousers and a long shirt, almost to his knees, and wearing a turban was operating a floor polisher, while another powerful-looking athletic man with the blackest skin she'd ever seen emptied the bins. Businesspeople rushed around, mostly talking on mobile phones but with earbuds in their ears.

Carmel went up to the desk and asked the Black woman who had multiple facial piercings and was wearing a vibrantly coloured hair-band how to get to Bedfordshire. Normally she hated asking people things, feeling like everyone else knew and she was making an eejit of herself by asking, but she had no choice.

'Bedfordshire is the county,' the woman explained kindly. 'You need to get to Bedford and from there to wherever you need to go.'

'Oh, right, em, thank you. How much is it?' Carmel asked, feeling the eyes of the two people who had queued up behind her boring into her neck. There was a money exchange in the Dublin port, so she'd changed the small amount of money she had into English pounds. She just hoped she had enough.

The woman tapped some keys on the computer and said, 'Six pounds, seventy one way, but there's a three-day return for eight pounds?'

'No. One way, please,' Carmel said with certainty, relieved she had enough to pay for it. Whatever happened now, she was never going back.

The woman tapped a few keys, and the machine spat out a ticket the size of a credit card. She slid it under the glass to Carmel. 'Bay 13, in twenty-five minutes.' She smiled and Carmel returned it. Maybe the world wasn't as scary as she thought it was. So far people had been friendly.

Carmel took her bag up once more and made her way to Bay 13. As she crossed the busy concourse, she noticed a bronze statue of a group of children and some suitcases. She stopped, wondering what it was about. There were boys and girls of all ages represented, and behind them a metal track like a train track. There were bronze suitcases and a violin case, and one of the children clutched a teddy bear. Around the plinth were the names of cities: Berlin, Prague, Leipzig, Vienna, Hamburg, Breslau.

'It's for the Kindertransport,' a heavy young woman in her twenties with a toddler in a buggy said as Carmel examined the statues.

'I'm sorry, I don't know...' Carmel flushed. The girl had purple hair and wore a voluminous Rolling Stones t-shirt. She spoke in the accent of London's East End, Carmel recognised it from a soap opera on TV.

'The kids that were allowed out of Germany, the Jews, before the war really got going. They arrived here, and their parents had no idea who was going to take care of them. I used to pass this every day going to work, but now that I have him' – she pointed to her sleeping child – 'I can never imagine how hard that must have been. Brave people.'

'Yes, they really were,' Carmel agreed.

'There's my bus – I better go. Bye,' the woman said, and then she was gone.

Carmel walked away from the statue, towards Bay 13. Something about that monument had given her a boost. If those parents and those little children could do it, let their little ones go, and those boys and girls could start again somewhere else, with no idea what the future held, then surely she could too.

The trip to Bedford took her out of the city, and she was surprised at how quickly the city ended and the green fields began. She asked again for directions to get to Aashna House and realised she could take a taxi as it wasn't that far. After a night of travelling, it was a relief to sit into the back of a car and be driven to her destination.

The taxi driver explained that it was outside the town and they drove away from the hustle and bustle. He stopped and indicated and turned left through some electric gates up an avenue bordered by well tended gardens either side. The main building was beautiful, an old house it looked like, but extensively modernised. Sometimes that can look incongruous, she liked those make over programmes on TV, but in the case of this place the new and the old blended seamlessly. It was one of the most beautiful places Carmel had ever seen.

Arriving to the reception of Aashna House, with her bag in her hand and no plan, was the most terrifying moment of her life. Standing outside as the taxi departed, she had to fight every urge in her body to run away. What if this was a horrible idea? She remembered watching a sitcom one time in which a couple were on holiday and made friends with another couple over pina coladas. They never expected their new friends to actually take them up on the offer to visit and pretended they weren't at home when the friends drove up to the house. Was that her now? She could feel her face burning to the tips of her ears at the thought. Was she the unwanted visitor?

She was just at the point of turning around when a distinguished elderly man came out of the large glass building atrium at the front of Aashna House and held the door open for her. She had no choice but to go in; to do otherwise would look mad.

'Good afternoon, how can I help?' The impeccably groomed young woman on the front desk smiled as she approached. She wore a name badge that said 'Marlena'. Carmel judged her to be in her late twenties, and she had a head of copper curls and dark-green eyes. She was petite and curvy, and Carmel could imagine her in an ad for something Irish, soap or perfume or those really expensive hand woven shawls that she'd never seen on anyone, though her accent was definitely British.

'I was hoping to speak to Dr Sharif Khan?' Carmel managed to croak.

'Do you have an appointment?' Marlena asked.

Carmel swallowed. 'Er...no. He...I...I met him recently and he said to contact him if I...' She heard her voice trial off. This was excruciating.

'No problem. What's your name? I'll pop him a message. He's around today, but he might be with a patient. Have a seat and I'll check.'

'It's Carmel Sheehan,' she said, barely audibly.

'Righto, just give me a sec.' The young woman smiled and picked up the phone on her desk. By the time Carmel sat down, she was too far away to hear what Marlena said.

The place was so serene and tastefully done. The reception was flooded with light from high glass ceilings at odd angles. On the floor were the most beautiful mosaic tiles, all in a palette of blues and greens. There were huge green plants that looked like they belonged in a jungle in colourful ceramic pots located all around the place. Photographs of people of all ages and colours hung on the walls, all smiling and happy. There was a coffee machine, and although she would have loved a hot drink after her long journey, she didn't dare.

'He's on his way,' Marlena called across the lobby and promptly answered another call.

Carmel felt her stomach lurch. She thought she might actually throw up.

'Carmel.' Sharif entered the reception from another door and walked towards her, arms outstretched.

She stood up and allowed herself to be embraced. He smelled just as he did in Dublin, a kind of citrus spice.

'How wonderful that you came. I was so sad when I read your note. I understood – well, sort of understood, but no matter. You're here now.'

He was genuinely thrilled to see her and she felt herself relax.

'I hope it's not a flying visit?' he said. 'Come up to my office. We can talk properly there.'

He led her to the glass elevator in the corner of the lobby and held a key card he had around his neck on a lanyard to the pad on the wall. The doors closed and the lift rose smoothly.

'No. I've left. For good. Whatever happens now, I won't be going back to Ballyshanley,' she said.

'Wonderful.' He grinned.

He took her down a deeply carpeted hallway that had a mezzanine overlooking the lobby below and opened a large dark wood door. 'Come in. Are you hungry? Thirsty? What can I get you?' He offered her a seat in the sunny office with a curved glass wall overlooking a beautiful garden.

'It's so beautiful here.' She breathed deeply, taking it all in.

'It is. We're lucky. It's a happy place. Now, have you eaten?' he asked again.

Normally she would say that she was fine, even though she was ravenous. 'I haven't actually,' she admitted.

'Right.' He grinned. 'First things first.' He lifted the phone. 'Marlena, can you ask someone to bring lunch for two to my office please?' There was a pause while she said something Carmel couldn't hear. Then Sharif put his hand over the receiver. 'Fish pie or vegetable curry or beef bourguignon?'

'Fish pie, please.' She smiled.

'Two fish pies, please, Marlena, and some desserts too and tea for two. Thanks. And can you hold all my calls, unless it's an emergency?'

He came to sit opposite her and without any hesitation took her hands in his.

CHAPTER 17

*I*t is so good to see you, Carmel, I can't describe. I'm so glad
you came.'

'I almost didn't about fifty times, but something spurred me on.'

'I'd like to think it was Dolly.' He winked, and her stomach felt like
there were a million butterflies fluttering about inside her.

She hadn't imagined it, and it wasn't the wine that night, or her
being star struck; he was every bit as attractive now as he was in
Dublin. He was wearing a charcoal-grey suit and a pale-pink shirt
under his white coat, and Carmel thought he looked amazing.

She gave him a brief rundown of the events leading up to her
departure and her journey there, and he told her about how his
mother had cried when he came home and told her that he'd found
Dolly's daughter.

They ate lunch and talked easily. Afterwards, Sharif gave her a tour
of the clinic. She glanced sideways as they walked, admiring him. He
caught her.

'I look different in my doctor outfit.' He grinned. When they'd met
in Dublin, he was dressed more casually. 'There's absolutely no clin-
ical reason whatsoever for it, but the residents feel more reassured
when I appear in my white coat with a stethoscope around my neck.'

He introduced her to people as they walked around. There were lots of staff and patients, who all stopped to greet Sharif as they wandered round the exquisite house and grounds, and she was struck by how familiar and relaxed they all seemed around him. In her limited experience, doctors were to be revered, along with priests, but everyone was relaxed and chatted and joked with Sharif. He was right, it seemed such a happy place, despite the fact that people came there to die. She met Zane, a care assistant; Oscar the yoga teacher; Ivanka, a tall, terrifyingly beautiful Swedish woman with the features of a goddess, who was an occupational therapist, though Carmel hadn't the faintest idea what that might be; and a cleaning lady called Ivy, who smoked like a chimney despite Sharif's admonishments. He had several conversations with patients they met, checking in with them and asking questions about their levels of comfort. Everyone seemed to love him.

Now that he was back in his own environment, she felt intimidated by his position. She didn't know anyone who'd been to university except Bill's girls and Julia, and the idea that someone as highly educated and successful as Sharif would want to associate with her made her feel a bit anxious, but she fought those feelings of inadequacy. It was just that sort of thinking that had let her waste away in Ballyshanley. Changing her surroundings was one thing, but she needed to change on the inside too.

The main house, behind the glass reception area, was the hospice itself. It was an old manor house, but while it maintained the grand façade of nineteenth-century opulence outside, inside it was transformed into bright airy spaces and cosy, exquisitely decorated private rooms. Each room was different, and while the medical technology employed was the most advanced, it was cleverly disguised so that each patient's room felt very homey.

Carmel remarked how it didn't smell like an institution. Sharif laughed and said every effort was made to use natural products for cleaning so there would be no offensively strong odours of disinfectant and the cooking was done in a separate building on the grounds. When possible, patients were encouraged to eat in the large bright glass-ceilinged atrium designed for that purpose over at the other end of the campus, but for those unable to, food was brought to them.

As well as various treatment rooms, there was a large multipurpose building, called Kaivalya, the Sanskrit word for unity, which Sharif explained was used for lectures, concerts and a variety of social events for the residents, and it was often used by local community groups as well. Sharif said that it was important that the people who came to Aashna didn't feel like they were withdrawing from the world, but instead remained part of it.

The lovely welcoming space overlooked the gardens with the lake in the middle and a fountain. Palliative care, he explained, was as much about mental health as about physical well-being. He'd visited several hospices all around the world before deciding on the format for Aashna House, and he declared with justified pride that there was nowhere like it.

'It must cost a fortune to stay here,' Carmel remarked. 'Are all the patients wealthy?'

Sharif shrugged. 'Some are, others not. We operate on a pay-if-you-can basis. The government subsidises us, and people can apply for waiving or reduction of fees. Those who can, pay, and we take everyone else on a case-by-case basis. I'm glad to say, though, that we're able to accommodate almost everyone who applies.'

'That sounds wonderful,' she said as she watched a man in his thirties push a bald woman in a wheelchair past them.

'Hi, Mary, how are you?' Sharif asked.

She nodded and the man placed his hand on her shoulder. 'Better now we got the double bed,' the woman said quietly. 'Don says the food's too good here, so he's staying.'

'That's the only reason.' The man winked.

They moved on and Sharif explained sadly, 'Mary is only thirty-five.'

'And can relatives stay too?' Carmel asked.

'Not usually, but she requested, and, well, it won't be for long, so we allow it sometimes.'

'I always thought of hospices as different to this.' Carmel looked around and took it all in. 'More like an institution or something or a hospital, but this place feels nothing like that.'

'That's the idea,' Sharif replied. 'Of course, I've had to beg and borrow for years to get it going – we started off with a much more modest place – but people are kind. Death is a universal reality, so perhaps people feel happy to donate in life with the hope that it is storing some kind of karma for their own inevitable end. Also we get a lot of bequests in people's wills. Though we never ask the residents, I hasten to add.' He chuckled. 'But people like to give back. And we've had a lot of government grants as well.'

'Well, a dumb priest never got a parish,' Carmel remarked, and Sharif gave a peal of laughter. 'What?' she asked, glad she had made him laugh.

'You're just like Dolly, so funny. She had the funniest sayings as well. She cracked me up and so do you.'

Just like when they met in Dublin, her Irishisms seemed to cause him no end of hilarity, and Carmel basked in his admiration.

As they walked through the gardens in the late spring sunshine, they came across an outdoor yoga class going on, with people of varying physical ability saluting the sun. They sat for a while on a bench and watched them. Carmel thought it would be so nice to try yoga, she had done one or two beginners classes using her phone and YouTube videos, but she was sure she was doing it all wrong.

'Do you do yoga?' she asked him.

'Daily.' He nodded. 'I've always done it, it's as much a part of my day as brushing my teeth, I can't imagine not spending some time on my mat every morning, good for the body, the mind and the soul.'

'I'd love to try it, but it looks so hard.'

'It's a practice, so there is no competition. Come to the class tomorrow if you like.'

After a bit, they continued with the tour. The accommodation section was mainly for resident staff and some patients who, while ill and in need of medical support, wanted to live out as much as possible of their time independently. There was also a family support section, where family members of very ill people could stay, cook a meal or watch TV. It really was a remarkable place.

'I don't know what I was expecting, but it wasn't this,' Carmel admitted as they sipped delicious creamy lattes in the on-site café.

'I know. I think people expect candles and hushed voices and a smell of boiled cabbage when they think of hospices. To be fair, very few are like that, but I do like to think Aashna is one of a kind. It's been my whole life's work. This place means the world to me. Now then, what would you like to do?' he asked.

'Well, in Dublin you kind of suggested I might work here, and I'd be very happy to do that. I'll do anything – cleaning, caring, whatever you need really. But if there are no vacancies, I understand.'

'I'd love you to join the team here,' he said, placing his hand on hers. 'I couldn't think of a single thing that would make me happier. Welcome to Aashna.'

'Thank you, Sharif. Thank you so much.' She tried to swallow the tears but couldn't. 'I've been so scared for so long...'

'Carmel, please, don't cry. This is a happy day. Let me tell you something. In the early days when I was setting up Aashna House, everyone said I was mad, that the place was costing too much, the furnishings and facilities were so top-end I'd never make my money back. They said that people wouldn't be able to afford to live here and I'd bankrupt myself. Even my parents were worried. But Dolly used to ask me, "What would you do if the fear was gone?" It is a great question to ask yourself, because once we remove the element of fear from our decisions, then we find our true heart's desire. Fear takes over if we let it, allowing people to only live half of the life they choose, or sometimes none of it, because they are crippled by terror and what ifs. So all over the world, people are staying in terrible marriages, awful jobs, living places they don't want to live, because they are afraid of what will happen if they take a leap of faith, they are afraid of their own instinct, and they lack trust in themselves. The old Carmel was like that, but you know who wasn't? Your mother, Dolly. She wasn't afraid of anyone or anything. She tried lots of things, never backed down when she knew she was right, and she would want this for you.

A new start, a chance to live your life on your terms, not somebody else's. I know she's gone, and it's so sad that you've never met her, but in a way, you have. Through me. So let her into your life. Let her guide you.' He paused and opened his mouth as if he were going to say something else but closed it again.

'Go on, say it, whatever you were going to say,' Carmel urged. 'I'd rather you were honest.'

'All right.' He exhaled. 'I want to say something, but even if it's wrong or I'm misreading things, then the offer of a job and place still stands, all right?'

'OK.' Carmel was confused now. What was he going to say?

'The thing is' – for the first time since she met him, he looked uncomfortable, awkward even – 'I'm so glad you came here, for you and for Dolly and all of that. I promised her I'd never give up, and I feel like I've fulfilled my promise. But something else happened in Dublin, something that has taken me completely by surprise. Since I left, I've not been able to get you out of my head. I've never been so attracted to anyone as I am to you, Carmel. Maybe it's because of Dolly or something, I don't know, but I can't help how I feel. I was very far beyond disappointed when I got your note in Dublin, and I cursed myself for not telling you how I felt that magical night, because I knew then. But I know with even more certainty now. Maybe I'm totally off the mark here, and please say so now before I make an even bigger fool of myself than I have already, but I just think that you are special, and kind and funny and so beautiful. And I have feelings for you. I can't stop thinking about you, and hoping that maybe you might feel the same. But maybe you are horrified, and I'm not the type of man who preys on vulnerable women, so please, if you don't think...well, just say it and we'll never discuss it again.' He swallowed.

The blood thundered in Carmel's ears. She thought this must be a dream. But it wasn't. 'I can't stop thinking about you either. But I never thought for a moment that anything could happen. I'm not that kind of person, and you're so successful and exotic and...'

Sharif laughed. 'Exotic? I've been called a lot of things, but never exotic.'

'Well, you are, to me anyway,' Carmel said, embarrassed.

'So I'm not wasting my time? I'm reading the signals correctly?' he asked, his head to one side, a smile playing on his lips.

'You are.' She smiled back, hardly daring to believe this was happening. 'But it's not that simple. Apart from anything else – and God knows there are a million reasons you shouldn't come near me with a barge pole – I'm a married woman.'

CHAPTER 18

Sharif sat back, running his fingers through his hair in exasperation. Then he leaned forward again and spoke conspiratorially. 'Carmel, you are never going back to Bill. Not because I say so, obviously, but because there is nothing to go back to. He doesn't love you – he told you that himself. He's obviously blind and deaf, but his loss is our gain. You tried your best, but you don't love him. You told me yourself that you were just a housekeeper. But let's speculate for a moment. Say you hate it here, you don't want me or Aashna or any of it, and you decide to leave here and get a job someplace else. Then would you be any worse off? Of course not. In fact, you'd still be much better off. You'd earn your own money, you'd have your own place, where you could just watch TV or have friends over or cook or whatever you want. So really, while this feels like a huge leap – I know it does – it's not, not in any real way.'

'I've never taken any leap, huge or otherwise.' Carmel smiled. 'But if by some miracle you are telling the truth and you want me to stay, then I can't think of anything I'd like more.'

* * *

AFTER THE COFFEE, Sharif opened the door to a lovely apartment. 'This is yours for as long as you want it,' he said, handing her the keys.

'But I can't...' she began. 'It's too much! Is there nowhere a bit more, well, modest? I've no money for rent, and this place must cost a fortune.'

'Carmel, please. Stop. This is part of your employment package.'

'Ah, Sharif, I can't. I'll get a small flat somewhere, or a room or something. Giving me a job is quite enough.'

He led her inside and stood before her. He was three or four inches taller, and she had to lift her chin to look in his dark almond shaped eyes.

'Carmel, I thought I'd never see you again. And now here you are. Please, let me do this, for you and for Dolly.'

The two-bedroomed apartment was the loveliest living space she'd ever seen, and Sharif assured her that she wasn't inconveniencing anyone by being there. There was a bright sunny ensuite master bedroom with a double bed and fitted wardrobes, and the bathroom had a huge shower and a deep Jacuzzi bath. The second bedroom was smaller but really cosy and decorated so nicely; it was like something she'd seen on those makeover programmes on TV. In awe, she wandered round touching surfaces. The lovely French doors opened onto a courtyard full of plants and shrubs, there were glittering black marble worktops, and there was an entertainment unit on one wall, which held the largest TV she'd ever seen. The living area was open-plan, with a kitchen, a sitting room with an oatmeal reclining sofa, and a dining table with four chairs. It was gorgeous, all creams and whites and a few splashes of colour here and there in rugs and prints.

Carmel had never in her whole life had a place of her own. She'd taken Sharif to see Trinity House, just from the outside, that day they'd walked around Dublin, and she had to admit that it looked quite dreary and forbidding. When she saw the dismay on his face that she had spent half of her life there, she'd tried to convince him that it wasn't that bad, not in comparison to some of the stuff heard about children who grew up in the care of the Catholic Church in Ireland, but she knew he was horrified. Despite her best efforts to make it sound less Orphan Annie, she knew her life story was pathetic, a life not lived, just endured year after year, with no hopes, plans or dreams. She tried to explain to him that she didn't feel so hopeless when she was in Trinity House, that it just was what it was and she knew no better. Some kids got parents and dogs and holidays and big extended families and others didn't, and she was one of the ones who didn't. She didn't feel self-pitying about it; it was how things were. Wishing for different was like wishing for a white blackbird.

Nobody had ever explained why she wasn't adopted; she just wasn't. But for some reason, Dolly was told she had been and that contact would be impossible. Carmel told Sharif how she wished so hard as a child to be picked by some family, taken home and loved like their own. It happened on TV, but it never seemed to be an option for her. As the years went on, the prospect became less and less likely. Other children left the home to go to families, but nobody ever showed the slightest interest in Carmel.

The reality of her situation as she wandered around her new home crashed over her like an icy wave. Panic threatened to engulf her. She'd only ever lived in two places, Trinity House and with Bill in County Offaly. What on earth had she been thinking, leaving everything she ever knew to just up sticks and land over here in England with a total stranger? She was worried that people here would look at her askance, wondering why the very eligible Dr Khan, who could have anyone he wanted, who owned and ran Aashna House, was showing a woman with no obvious skills around and moving her into this amazing apartment.

As he showed her the coffee machine, his beeper went off. He read it and apologised. 'I'm sorry, a patient needs me. Can I leave you here to settle in? Unpack and so on? I'll come and find you when I'm free. Please feel free to wander around.'

'Of...of course...sure.' She tried not to panic.

He went to the door and then turned back. He stood in front of her, his hands on her shoulders. 'I can't tell you how happy I am to see you. Please don't worry – everything is going to be fine now.' He kissed her cheek and was gone.

She sat down on the beautiful sofa and tried to focus on her breathing. *Calm*, she told herself, *just try to be calm. In and out, in and out.* Gradually, her heartbeat returned to normal.

She looked out on the large lawn in front of the apartment block, filled with patients and their families on such a sunny day. The residents were not all in bed as she imagined they would be. Sharif explained how the ethos of Aashna was that people should suck the marrow out of life, enjoy it, experience new things as much as they were able and not just sit around waiting to die. Most were busy with various activities – painting, yoga, book clubs, even brewing beer.

She tried to recline on the sofa in her first very own apartment as the sun streamed through the glass doors but was afraid to relax, full sure someone would appear any moment and demand to know who on earth she thought she was. The glass-topped table had a vase of yellow crocuses on it, and Carmel tried to imagine a future where she would cook in her little kitchen and have friends sit at the table and eat a meal as her guests. She'd have to find a few friends first, she reminded herself ruefully.

There was a large glass and enamel mirror over the fireplace, and she stood to assess the woman looking back at her. The mirror was nothing like the awful oval one in Bill's house, with the curly metal bits and spotted glass. Like everything here, it was shiny and new.

She thought she looked every one of her forty years. Crow's feet radiated from her big blue eyes. The reflection confirmed what she suspected, that her dark shoulder-length hair made her look like a ghost. The stress of recent times had caused her to lose weight, and her spare tyre had just melted away. In fact, she thought she looked kind of gaunt. She should never have allowed Julia to talk her into dying her blonde hair brown. She felt discordant, like she didn't fit herself or something. She could hear her sister-in-law's sharp voice in her head. 'Less conspicuous, the dark. Blond can look very trashy. A nice brown colour to hide the grey – that's much better.'

Carmel had hated her brown hair the moment she saw it all those years ago, but to go against Julia once she'd issued a decree took more strength than she'd ever possessed. Maybe now she could allow her hair to return to its natural colour. Could she do that? Would she?

She wondered what was happening back in Ballyshanley. She was afraid to look at her phone.

She thought back to the conversation with Sharif earlier in the hospice café. The whole sorry tale of the confrontations with Julia and Bill came out in a torrent, and she was mortified when the tears started up again. He'd reached over the table and held her hand, not caring who saw them.

She replayed the scene in her mind as she sat on the sofa, watching a little robin at the bird bath in the tiny courtyard. Sharif was right; no matter what, there was no going back now. Even if she wanted to, Bill and Julia would probably see her off with the shotgun after what she'd done.

CHAPTER 19

*C*armel's reverie was interrupted by Zane giving her a wave as he passed the window. When she'd met him briefly with Sharif, he was funny and spoke with a real East End London accent. He was so stylish, with his skinny jeans with the frayed ends, snow-white sneakers and skintight shirt showing off his well-toned body. His hair was shaved on both sides and sporting a full Afro on the top, and as Sharif introduced them, she tried not to stare. It was the first conversation she'd ever had with a Black person. He would have looked like a mysterious tropical bird in a flock of boring grey pigeons in Ballyshanley, but over here, he was just part of the wonderfully colourful tapestry of life.

Everything in England was so different. Sure, in Ireland there were more and more immigrants, but nothing like the huge crossroads of the entire world she saw here. Sharif had laughed when he caught her gazing in amazement at a group of Muslim teenage girls with hijabs covering their heads but wearing expensive sportswear on their bodies. They were having a loud argument in the garden as they passed. One of them was in a wheelchair, and several others were crowded around her, clearly in disagreement over something.

She waved back at Zane and smiled. Maybe everything was going to be OK.

She'd switched her phone off when she got on the boat – it felt kind of symbolic or something – but now she knew she'd have to at least check her messages. Fighting feelings of dread, she pressed the 'on' button. Sharif had given her the password, so Carmel connected to the Wi-Fi, and within seconds her phone buzzed several times.

The first message was from Niamh. *Carmel, what the hell do you think you are doing? Dad is devastated. I can't believe U R being so selfish after all we've done for you. N*

The next text was from Sinead, who had always been the nicer of the two, though Carmel never really got close to either girl despite her very best efforts. *Carmel, are you OK? Please ring. We're all worried about you. Dad especially.*

One from Julia. *You are a ridiculous woman. You came from nothing and you'll go back to nothing. Bill foolishly thought he could normalise you, but it proved impossible. We are all better off without you.*

Another from Niamh, presumably sent when Carmel didn't answer the first one. *Carmel, do not attempt to enter our home again. You're no longer welcome there. You have broken my father's heart, you horrible ungrateful cow. You're lucky we won't press charges for you trying to kill our Auntie Julia.*

Carmel could just hear Julia on the phone, weaving her tale of woe to the girls, painting Carmel as the villain of the piece, no doubt.

Carmel sighed and deleted each text in turn. Nothing from Bill; he hadn't tried to phone or send a text. He didn't have a mobile phone, possibly the last person on earth to hold out against the new-fangled technology, and she knew he'd never lift the receiver on the phone on the wall in the kitchen and punch in the number. The fact that he would have no idea of her phone number said enough really. He didn't speak when they were face to face, so he would certainly never consider a phone chat. And Carmel knew that despite what Julia and the girls had said, she had not broken his heart and he most certainly was not devastated.

She wondered if anyone in Ballyshanley would miss her, or even notice she was gone. The gossip machine would start up soon and Bill would be embarrassed, but the people would reassure him that he was better off and that Carmel was damaged goods and that nobody who came out of an institution was right in the head. 'Just listen to the radio any day,' she could hear them say in the pub and the post office. 'All those people who came out of homes and industrial schools – it's very sad, but they all have drink and drug problems and they can't make relationships work. 'Tis not their fault, God knows, but they aren't suitable matches for normal people.'

She turned the phone off again and threw it in her bag. Well, that was that.

Someone had placed milk and tea and some groceries in the fridge, so she made a cup of tea. Did she really do that? Just pack a bag, walk into Ballyshanley, get the bus to Dublin and from there cross the Irish Sea to here? And now she was sitting in her own gorgeous apartment, making herself a cup of tea. Surely that couldn't be right. She was the one who left her marriage; she was the villain of the piece. How come things had worked out so well for her?

She wondered if Bill just got up and went out to the farm the next morning after she left. Did he make his own breakfast? What did he think about her sudden and unprecedented disappearing act? Did Julia tell him about the fight?

She was so grateful she'd had a passport. Even getting a passport with the birth certificate supplied by the home was such a sad experience. Her father was marked as unknown and her mother just as 'Mary Murphy'. Carmel often wondered who Mary was and if Murphy even was her real name.

She remembered when Kit got her passport; her mother was listed as Mary Murphy as well. They thought for a minute they might be sisters, but Sister Margaret explained that most unmarried mothers were listed as Mary Murphy to protect their identity.

The little wine-coloured book with the gold harp on the front had remained pristine in the drawer beside her bed since before Niamh got married. She liked to read the message inside, where the Minister for Foreign Affairs asked that the bearer, a citizen of the Republic of

Ireland, be offered all assistance necessary to travel within other countries. She knew it was silly, but it made her feel part of something. She wasn't in a family really and she didn't have any real friends, but she was an Irish citizen and the minister cared about her.

She wondered if she should offer to pay for the groceries. She had a little money left from the coal money. She didn't have any bank cards; Bill took care of everything. There was an account at the local shop, so she got what she needed and he settled up the bill at the end of the month. She didn't drive, so there was nothing else really. She had her phone, which she loved. She saved up three Christmas vouchers to pay for it. She would have loved an iPhone, but it was too dear.

For twenty euros a month, she could send and receive texts, though she had nobody to text, but more importantly, she could surf the net. She'd had to siphon the twenty euro off the spare change Bill left around, and she felt awful doing it but it would never occur to him to give her any money and he wouldn't like her to work, so she had no choice. She learned how to use the internet quickly and joined lots of groups online, all on the themes of mindfulness and spirituality. She also downloaded apps that gave guided meditations and listened to all those American gurus who said to go out and live your best life.

She might have ignored their message up to this, she thought as she sipped her tea and wrapped her hands around the mug, but something must have sunk in because she was here and she'd done it.

CHAPTER 20

*C*armel unpacked her few belongings and took a shower. She dressed in a red top she'd bought in a charity shop for two euro but that Julia had seen in the bag and scoffed at, telling her it was much too young for her. Defiantly she put it on; it was nice on her.

Of Sharif there was still no sign, and the afternoon had turned to evening. She felt a bit silly setting the table for herself, just to have another cup of tea and a cheese sandwich, but she tried to channel her inner Oprah, who would tell her to enjoy the drink and sandwich, focus on it, really taste it and experience it. All of that sounded like a load of old rubbish to her at the start, but the more she got into the whole mindfulness thing, the more it made sense to her. She sat at the table in this beautiful peaceful place and counted her blessings. She was healthy and had an envelope full of letters her birth mother had written to her over the years, she was wearing a necklace and earrings her mother had left for her, and she now had Dr Sharif Khan in her corner. Initially, he was fulfilling a promise he made to Dolly, but when they met in Dublin that day, something happened. It was as if he saw her, really saw her, like nobody else had ever done before. He had feelings for her; those were his words. Inconceivable as it might seem, she thought he was telling the truth. He was an unusual man by anyone's standards, not just in her limited life experience. His mesmerising eyes, the brows that looked so perfectly shaped it was as if they had been done in a salon, his slightly flared nostrils, his skin the colour of the latte he bought for her in the café. He reminded her of a panther or a tiger or one of those cats that moved powerfully but with such grace. But his personality too was unlike anyone she'd ever met. He wasn't embarrassed when he cried. He was intense, but there was a depth of kindness to him; she could see it not just with how he spoke to her but to his patients too. He was able to sit in discomfort; he didn't need to fill the space or try to do the Irish thing of 'sure it could be worse'. He wasn't afraid to say what he thought. Even the way he spoke about death wasn't euphemistically, as she'd been used to, whisperings about passing away. He spoke matter-of-factly but with compassion. It was an odd but intriguing mix. Dolly was absolutely right – he was a special man.

That night over dinner in Dublin, and later back at the hotel, he told her more about her mother, about what a character she was. He told her about his own parents, his mother's friendship with hers. He listened to her stories about growing up in Trinity House. She told him about the last letter from Kit, asking if Carmel was in a John B Keane play when she heard about her engagement. Kit had ranted that Bill was ancient, thirty-seven to her twenty-three, claiming it was more like something from the '50s than the '90s. But it was an offer and Carmel hadn't had any of those. Carmel never knew if Kit read her reply, full of hurt and pain at what she saw as her friend's betrayal. She hoped she never got it.

She explained to Sharif that it was the bravest thing she'd ever done, agreeing to marry Bill. Nobody was interested, though, and even the nuns thought she was mad, but she couldn't stay at Trinity House forever. She spent the weeks before the wedding imagining a life where she had a husband and two adorable little girls calling her Mammy. She would have friends who also had families, and they'd talk about how their husbands' snoring was driving them crazy or how their little one was getting on at piano lessons. In truth, Carmel hadn't a clue what married people talked about, but she imagined it was something along those lines. She couldn't wait. But it turned out that the nuns were right, that it was a mad idea, a gamble that most certainly did not pay off.

As she finished off her delicious sandwich and drank her tea gratefully, there was a gentle knock on the door. She jumped as if she had no right to be there, but then stood and opened the door and tried not to look like a rabbit caught in the headlights.

'Hello, you. Wow, you look gorgeous in that top. Settled in OK?' Sharif stood outside. 'May I come in?'

She stood back to allow him in, which she knew was ridiculous; he owned the whole place, for God's sake. As with every time she looked at him, the breath caught in her throat. He really was beautiful. She knew that wasn't a word usually attributed to men, but Sharif Khan was beautiful. He looked like one of those models for coffee or expensive aftershave she'd seen in the magazines at the hairdresser's. She blushed pink at the thought that he could read her mind and tried to cover it up with a discreet cough, which turned into a wheezing fit. She really had to pull herself together.

He handed her a glass of water and waited for her to recover her composure. 'Do you have an inhaler? For your asthma?' he asked, suddenly the doctor, not the rescuer.

'No,' she wheezed. 'It's not too bad. Much better than when I was a kid. I can manage.' She tried to make her breathing sound less laboured. She had had trouble with wheezing since she was a child, but nobody had ever diagnosed it as asthma before.

'But you do have an inhaler?' he asked.

'No, never. I just manage it myself,' she said on the exhale.

'Sit,' he commanded, leading her to the chair. Removing his stethoscope from his neck, he put it in his ears and raised up her top, placing the cold part on her back. He moved it to several spots and did the same on her chest. 'Are you seriously telling me that you have had this condition since childhood and you have never used medication? Carmel, do you have any idea what damage you have done to your lungs? Each asthma attack scars your lungs and puts your heart under undue pressure, and really there is no need. I'll write you a prescription for a preventative and an inhaler for when you are having an attack. Take it to Rosa over at the pharmacy – it's beside the reception. You take the preventative morning and evening and the other as you need it.'

He went to his medical bag he'd left by the door and opened it, rooting inside, returning moments later with a grey-blue inhaler. 'OK, sit on the couch, open your mouth, and suck in when I press.'

'Yes, Doctor.' She grinned.

He administered the medicine, and within seconds her chest felt less tight. It was amazing.

'And again,' he said, and she did as she was told but shrugged off his stethoscope as he tried to listen to her chest again.

'I can see you are not going to be a good patient.' He chuckled. 'Just like your mother. She was impossible, smoked cigarettes to the day she died, had gin and tonics every night, loved Kentucky Fried Chicken and organised a take-out night here every Friday where the residents had too much alcohol and a fairly savage poker school. I'm going to have my work cut out for me with you too, as she would say.'

'Thank you,' she said quietly.

The way Sharif drew her mother into the conversation so regularly and so unselfconsciously had made her squirm at first. It raised uncomfortable truths for her. But he kept on doing it, and as each hour passed, Dolly Mullane became a real person.

Carmel had copied and reduced in size the photos her mother had left her – one of her and a man called Joe, another of Sharif's family, another of her at her birthday party, the last one before she died – and the smaller versions were now tucked into Carmel's wallet; she must have examined them a hundred times.

'What for?' he asked as he hung his stethoscope round his neck once more.

'Everything.' Carmel spread her arms around. 'This apartment, offering me a job, finding me. All of it.'

'No regrets?' he asked quietly. He sat beside her on the couch and drew her head onto his shoulder, putting his arm around her gently. It felt instantly comfortable. She loved the physical proximity of him.

'No, no regrets. Terror at the future, yes. Worry about, well...
everything, definitely. But regrets, no. That life is gone now, for better
or worse. They texted me, his daughters, Julia, accusing me of
breaking his heart. The reality, though, is I doubt he even noticed I
was gone. Julia has probably moved in – she wanted that when Gretta
died. She never married herself, you see. Allegedly, she used to
harbour hopes for Donald Wooton, the local landowning bigwig. He
might have flirted a bit or something, but everyone in the place had it
that she was carrying a torch for him. At least she was until he up and
married some Protestant he met at the races in Leopardstown, with a
big farm of land and a plummy accent. Maybe she thinks if she gets
her hands on Bill's farm, she'll have men queuing up for her, though I
doubt it. Anyway, to answer your question, how could I have second
thoughts about this place? It's so beautiful.'

'And me? Any second thoughts about that?' Suddenly, all the self-
assuredness disappeared. He wasn't the very wealthy, capable doctor
but just a vulnerable man.

She turned and looked up into his face, placing a hand on his chest.
'Of course I haven't. You're the one who should be running a mile.
Seriously, Sharif, I've nothing. I've no skills. I don't know anyone or
anything. I don't know what on earth you'd want to hitch your very
fancy wagon to me for – honest to God, I don't. I'm about as useful as
an ashtray on a motorbike, and for all I know, I could be a wanted
criminal back in Ireland for shoving that angular old bat down the
stairs.'

He threw back his head and laughed; the sight of it never ceased to
delight her. 'I can just picture it. Well done. Sounds like she deserved
it. Anyway, you said she got up again, so she's fine. And as for you
being useful, well, just leave that to me, OK? You forget, to me you are
someone very special indeed, not just because I've met you and know
you to be a hilarious, charming, beautiful woman, but because in some
ways I feel like I've always known you. Dolly talked about you all the
time, spent hours speculating how you would be. She would look at
pictures in the Irish papers of people at parties or the races or even on
the Irish news, and she would scan the street crowds when they did

outside broadcasts. I'd lost count of the number of times she'd pause it and call me, asking if I thought this woman or that one was you.'

Carmel grinned at the thought; it elated her. 'You're making her real for me – not just a memory, but an actual person.'

'Oh, she was real all right, larger than life...and you're her daughter.'

He sat up and held her face between his two hands. His eyes searched hers. Her heart thumped so wildly she was sure he could hear it. Her mouth was dry, but she didn't want to swallow and betray just how nervous she was.

His lips on hers were cool at first, and the slight bristle on his face tickled her. She felt herself responding to him, wanting to crawl inside him almost and never have to face the world alone again. On and on he kissed her, their mouths opening, their tongues exploring, and Carmel knew that this first kiss of her life, at forty years of age was the one worth waiting for.

She wrapped her arms around him, holding him close, and she could hear his heart beating. He held her tightly, and they kissed on and on as the moon rose in the inky sky.

CHAPTER 21

*C*armel glanced at her watch. Ten to nine. The meeting was at nine, and she didn't want to arrive too early in case she was left standing alone, feeling awkward. Sharif had resisted at first, telling her he wanted her to relax and take it easy for a few days at least, but she wanted to get busy. Eventually she pestered him, pleaded with him to find her something useful to do until he gave in. She had been stunned when he suggested a role for her. She'd imagined a cleaning job or something. But instead she was now the official events coordinator at Aashna House. He offered her the position, explaining that the woman who used to do it called from Portugal last week, where she was on holiday, to say she was staying there with the love of her life, a twenty-four-year-old Syrian waiter she'd met in a disco. Sharif explained that this development had caused a few raised eyebrows from the other staff, given that Maureen was fifty if she was a day, but they had a whip-round and wished her well. Sharif was more understanding than most employers would have been, and when Carmel asked him about it, he just said that Maureen had not always had things easy, so if this man gave her some joy, then who was he to stand in the way?

'But what if he's just using her to get a passport?' Carmel asked from the kitchen, where she was preparing a snack.

It felt so relaxed, the two of them, chatting happily. Sharif had kicked his shoes off and was sitting cross-legged on the floor. At first, she had smiled at the peculiar pose, but he explained that he spent most of his downtime sitting like that – it was a Pakistani thing – and it was his most comfortable position. He explained how sitting cross-legged on the floor was in fact a Yoga asana known as sukhasana, which aided digestion and encouraged mindfulness.

That first night they spent together, her first night in Aashna House, felt like the most natural thing in the world. Carmel never imagined lovemaking to be like it was with Sharif, gentle, passionate and fun. She was in love for the first time. She couldn't imagine ever being happier than this.

She'd mentioned in Dublin that she and Bill had never consummated their marriage, but Sharif had assumed that she'd had other boyfriends, so she'd had to tell him that she was a complete novice. She knew the mechanics, obviously, but what one was actually supposed to do was a bit vague. She even told him about her botched attempt at seduction that horrific night with Bill. Sharif let her talk and then held her tight and assured her that if she'd gone to that much trouble for him, he would have had a very different reaction. After that, it was easy.

'Well, if he is, he is,' Sharif said. 'But from what she said, he's a refugee, lost all his family in the flight from the war, and Maureen is not only remarkably good-looking and well presented for her age, but there's an inherent kindness in her. Maybe he sees that too and needs her as much as she needs him. She seems convinced he's genuine, and I'd trust her judgement.'

'You're lovely,' she said, and kissed him on the nose as she placed the plate of cheese and crackers and a glass of wine down in front of him.

'You are quite lovely yourself.' He grinned as he pulled her down to sit with him, kissing her neck as she leaned back against him.

She had taken the job gladly and tried to figure out what exactly an events coordinator did. Sharif said not to worry too much, that

Maureen had left a filing cabinet full of contacts and a schedule of events on her desk in the office that Carmel had now inherited. It all had happened so quickly. She'd been there only a few short days, but it felt much longer.

Eventually she took a deep breath to steady herself, pushed the door of the Kaivalya and entered the auditorium, trying to look approachable, friendly and competent. The more mobile of the residents shuffled into the sunny area and took their seats. Some were pushed on wheelchairs by staff, and others were assisted by visiting relatives. Everyone settled in to hear her first address as coordinator. She was quaking but determined to do her best. Sharif had offered to come, but she said it might be best just to go it alone. He couldn't hold her hand forever, and she wanted people to see her as a member of the staff, not Sharif's girlfriend.

'G-good morning everyone and thanks for coming...' Oh God, she sounded like a rubbish comedian. 'I...I don't mean thanks for coming here, obviously, as you are here already, but for coming to listen to me, though this is where you all come every day...'

She was babbling and she knew it; her nerves were getting the better of her. She stopped and took a deep breath. 'I'm sorry, I'll start again. I'm not used to speaking to people like this. I think I've met some of you already, but just to introduce myself, my name is Carmel, Carmel Mullane, and some of you may remember my mother, Dolly.' Though this was a hospice and so people didn't come to stay for that long, Sharif did mention to her that some of the residents were there when Dolly was.

There was excited nudging and whispering. She was still getting used to introducing herself as Carmel Mullane rather than Sheehan. Since she'd never felt like part of Bill's family anyway, it seemed stupid to keep his name. This time, her name meant something to her; she was her mother's daughter, and she had the name her mother gave her.

'So it's true that Dr Khan found you? You're baby Carmel?' A very elderly lady with snow-white hair and intelligent green eyes spoke up in a strong cockney accent.

'Yes, I suppose I am. Though that was forty years ago. I never knew she was looking for me. I wish I had – maybe we would have found each other before it was too late.' Carmel heard her voice crack with emotion.

Seeing her vulnerability seemed to melt the crowd, and within moments, they had moved forward and were welcoming her warmly.

'Well, we're glad you're here, Carmel. I know it would have meant the world to Dolly – you were all she talked about.' A heavyset old man with a Welsh accent spoke up from a motorised wheelchair. 'Most of the people here will have heard of Dolly even if they didn't meet her. She was a good sort, old Dolly, always up to some kind of mischief.' He chuckled.

That comment seemed to bring general agreement from the gathered crowd.

Encouraged by their welcome, Carmel went on. 'So Dr Khan has asked me to take over from Maureen. I'm really happy to do it, but I must tell you that I'm new to all of this. I understand that I am responsible for organising activities, speakers, trips out, classes and so on for anyone interested. I have the regular schedule, but if I miss out on anything, or there is something you'd like added, please let me know and I'll try to organise it.'

The rest of the morning flew by as she spoke to people individually, asking them what kinds of activities they were interested in. Some people were too ill to even consider courses or concerts, but a surprising number of people were able and wanted something to fill the days. One lady called Claire confided in Carmel that she had no idea that she had any aptitude for landscape painting until she came to the hospice. The painting classes on Tuesdays and Fridays were a big hit. 'Imagine' – she smiled – 'I might have made a fortune had I known sooner.'

Two old ladies called Sheila and Kate took her to the window to show her the bird feeders they had built for the garden, each one with different sized apertures to attract different birds.

Sharif had explained when they spotted Sheila and Kate sitting together in the garden on the day Carmel arrived that the women were gay and lifelong partners. They'd been together for almost fifty years. When Sheila was diagnosed with stage three lung cancer, Kate cared for her at home until her needs became too complex. They visited Aashna House and decided it was the best place for her. It broke their hearts to be separated, and for the first few months, Kate would appear before breakfast and not leave until after Sheila had gone to bed. One night, the weather outside was treacherous and Sharif suggested a bed be put in Sheila's room and Kate stay over. She stayed that night and every night since. Nobody mentioned it, and since everyone had a private room, many patients never even noticed. Sheila and Kate were so happy to be reunited, and their infectious enthusiasm and stories of London in the swinging '60s entertained the residents that had few visitors. They knew everyone back in the day and dropped names of film stars and musicians effortlessly. The pair still dressed like they were hanging around Carnaby Street, in tie-dyed caftans and beads.

Slowly she was coming to grips with everything and the cast of colourful characters that made up Aashna delighted her. There was an acceptance here, of lifestyle, of race, of culture, that she never knew existed in the world, nobody judged anyone and it was so refreshing.

Carmel had spoken to Oscar about the yoga classes he held every day at ten thirty and four thirty and was amazed at how many residents attended, even though many were very ill indeed. She had to concentrate hard to understand Oscar. He was from Aberdeen in Scotland, and though he told her he'd lived down south for many years now, he spoke like he'd left Aberdeen yesterday.

'Sometimes,' Oscar explained, 'it might be as simple as facing the wheelchair to the sun and the person raising their arms or even just their hands in a sun salute, while there are others who are able do stretches and poses. Yoga isn't about how much you can do, how far you can stretch, but everyone who does it benefits from it – I really believe that. On sunny days, we try to do it outside. It can take some organising with mats and chairs and all of that, but it's lovely to hear the birds as we do our practice.'

Carmel instantly warmed to the man. He was wiry and thin, with a long grey ponytail and rimless glasses. He smelled of sandalwood and wore loose-fitting clothes. He looked to be in his fifties, but his face was unlined and he looked so fit and flexible, it was hard to be sure.

'How long have you been teaching yoga?' she asked.

'Oh, not that long. I'm a late bloomer. I started doing it to de-stress. That's where I met Sharif, actually. He's been practising for years. We got talking at a local yoga studio one day. I used to be an investment banker, lived hard, played hard, drinking, drugs you name it, then an enormous deal I arranged went sour and some very powerful people lost a lot of money. I had a nervous breakdown from the stress of it all and ended up in a psychiatric unit after I went crazy and broke up the house. My wife at the time had to call the police – I was out of control. I spent three months in hospital and a full year in daily therapy and part of that was practising yoga every day. That was nine years ago.' He smiled, clearly at peace with his past. 'You should come along to a class – you'd be more than welcome.'

There had been an ad up in the shop for classes starting in the community centre in Ballyshanley a year or so ago, but when she mentioned it to Bill, he said they were probably all drug-taking hippies and she'd be better not to be seen mixing with them.

'Well, I'd love to try – I've wanted to for ages actually – but I'm supposed to be working, so I don't know...'

'Oh, don't worry about that. A lot of the staff join in. It's something we encourage for everyone. Often Sharif joins us or his mum, Nadia – have you met her yet?'

'Er...no, not yet. She's away, visiting some relatives in Pakistan.' Carmel tried to hide the trepidation in her voice. She was dreading meeting Nadia; the woman would most likely be horrified that her eligible, successful son had hooked up with someone like her.

'Oh, that's right. She'll be back soon, though. You'll like her – she's great. Anyway, I best crack on. We are going to try downward dog today with a man who has had extensive back surgery to remove several tumours, but he's determined to try. See you around and welcome to the team, Carmel.'

CHAPTER 22

*E*veryone at the meeting was warm and friendly, if a little curious. After Carmel met the patients, she ran into Ivy, who was finishing the vacuuming and invited her for a cup of tea. Carmel instantly warmed to the chubby, short woman with the accent straight off *EastEnders*, the soap opera set in London she used to watch. As they sipped tea and shared a slice of a Valencia orange cake, Ivy told Carmel some more stories of Dolly. Carmel couldn't help but laugh at the antics her mother got up to while she was in Aashna.

'There was this one time she arranged a kissogram for the birthday of an old retired schoolteacher who was a very uptight and strait-laced geezer.' Ivy was a natural storyteller. 'But when the kissogram turned up, it turned out to be one of the young teachers on the staff of his old school making a few extra quid at the weekends. Both of them were horrified but locked in a code of silence. Nobody in the staff knew the elderly man was sick and he certainly didn't want it known, and she's have probably got the boot from the new principal if they found out about her part time job, so they both had to keep shtum.' Ivy's laughter at the memory caused her to go into a coughing fit.

'I know I keep saying it, but I wish I'd met her,' Carmel said sadly, handing Ivy a glass of water.

The other woman nodded. 'Well, she's here, Carmel. She can see you and hear you. I can tell you that. You don't work with the dying as long as I have and not know there's more to it than this.'

'Do you really think so?' Carmel asked, intrigued.

Ivy nodded. 'If you ask anyone who works in a hospice or a hospital or old-folks home or something, they'll tell you the same thing. There's a kind of, I don't know, a peace or a knowing or something that comes over people. Religious and not, Black and White, rich and poor – it doesn't matter. They come in here, sad, sick, depressed, all of that. But living here, whether for a week or a month or a year, changes them. It gives them that way of leaving, dignified, happy-like, on their own terms. Sharif sets the example and everyone else follows, but there's something else. People know towards the end. It's as if the other life, whatever waits for us all on the other side, comes closer and the person isn't scared any more.'

'I love that idea,' Carmel said softly.

'Are you religious?' Ivy asked.

Carmel shrugged. 'Well, I was raised a Catholic and I used to go to Mass every Sunday and all of that, but I don't know that I ever really connected with it on a personal level. I like the idea of it, though, of there being a spirituality to people, that we all have an essence or a soul or whatever.'

Ivy nodded. 'I think that's it. We get all sorts in here, atheists, Christians of all kinds, Hindus, Muslims, Jews. You name it, we've had them. And when you see everyone together, facing the exact same fate that awaits us all sooner or later, it teaches you something.'

'What's that?' Carmel asked, intrigued.

'That we're all the same, and nobody knows for sure what comes next, no matter how much they claim they do. But there is something, my dear, of that you can be certain.' She patted Carmel's hand. 'So don't waste time feeling sad you never got to speak to your mum. Talk to her now. She can hear you, and if you listen carefully, you can hear her too. Someone who burned as bright as your mum did, she'll stick around for a bit.' She chuckled. 'Now I'm off outside for a quick puff before I go home, but don't tell Sharif or I'll be getting another lecture.' She rolled her eyes theatrically and put her coat on.

'I won't,' Carmel promised with a smile. 'And thanks for telling me about my mum.'

'You're the image of her, you know? I expect everyone tells you that.' Ivy smiled as she walked away.

Carmel sat in contented silence as the harmonious world of Aashna House hummed around her.

CHAPTER 23

The weeks flew by, and Carmel really got into the swing of the job. She worked Monday to Friday, barely seeing Sharif all day, but every evening they had dinner together and slept each night wrapped around each other. Sometimes she woke and just watched him sleeping. She was so in love that it terrified her. In the small hours of the morning, she felt undeserving of such joy and feared it must surely be short-lived. People didn't live like this, did they? In love, comfortable, fulfilled in their work? It all felt too much after a lifetime of deprivation. Trinity House, Ballyshanley, Bill and Julia – it all felt like another lifetime ago.

He told her more about her mother, never in an orchestrated or contrived way, just as it came up in conversation. They talked about the hospice and the people who stayed there, and she was constantly impressed at how personally Sharif took his work.

He was fulsome in his praise for her management of events and delighted with her idea of a suggestion box for events because some people might feel self-conscious about asking her to put on particular activities, unsure if others would like them or not. She devised a system that no matter how outlandish the suggestion, if it got three votes, then it would be added to the suggestion whiteboard that week. If enough people put a tick beside it, then she sourced a teacher.

Next week they had a falconry expert coming and bringing his birds of prey, and the following week, there was a barbershop quartet coming to give a harmony singing class. It had become a kind of challenge for the residents to come up with unusual requests, and she loved the banter it generated. She spent a lot of each day on the phone to complete strangers, making arrangements, and it didn't faze her as much as it used to. She stammered less in conversation and found she loved just popping into the café during the day for a cup of tea or a snack and chatting to whoever was there.

At the weekends, they explored, Sharif driving her around to see the sights in his vintage Jaguar. Like him, the car was quirky. It was a 1969 Jaguar 240 in pale blue with chrome trim. He loved it and she did too. It smelled of leather, and while it didn't go as fast as modern cars, it drew admiring glances everywhere they went. A bit like its owner, she had to admit. Sharif was happy to answer questions about it, and regularly they found themselves in conversations with classic-car enthusiasts.

One weekend they took the train to London and stayed at the Ritz Hotel. It was so gorgeous, and the architecture and history just astounded her. She loved the anonymity of that city, people just accepting all the diversity of mankind and getting on with their own lives. Sharif really enjoyed showing his city to her; he loved London and knew so much about it. In Brick Lane, they ate curries so hot they almost blew the top of her head off, though Sharif had no problems, and on Saturday morning they took a walking tour to see the street art of the city. She saw paintings by the famous but enigmatic Banksy, and she was mesmerised by the skill of the graffiti artists.

She couldn't believe she was actually there, in places she'd only seen on TV, and yet there she was, looking up at St Paul's, crossing over Tower Bridge, seeing the changing of the guard at Buckingham Palace. She and Sharif were sitting outside a café at Piccadilly Circus when Prince Charles and Camilla passed by in their car. Carmel nearly squealed with excitement. Slowly, England was feeling like home, and she just loved it.

Her first month's salary seemed a gigantic amount of money, but Sharif assured her it was the same salary as Maureen had received before she left. Carmel had never earned any money before and was totally ill-equipped to deal with spending it. The day Sharif took her to open her first bank account, he waited outside while she went in. She didn't want to seem like a total eejit, having never had a reason to even be in a bank before, apart from once or twice dropping in a letter to the manager of Allied Irish Banks in Ballyshanley for Bill.

The lady in the bank offered her a selection of plastic cards, a Visa debit or credit card, but she refused, remembering how Bill always said 'cash is king' and plastic cards were the slippery slope to ruination. When Sharif heard that once she emerged, he gently sent her back into the branch to ask for a debit card. They'd thought it odd that she didn't want one in the first place, and assured her it would be in the post in a few days. Her heart almost burst with pride when they asked her for her address. To have an apartment number, one of her very own, and a place to call hers meant so much to her, in a way that nobody could understand.

The 188 euro meant for the coal back in Ballyshanley had lasted her the entire month. Sharif offered, on more than one occasion, to give her an advance, but she refused. Once she got paid, she went into the bank and changed that exact amount from sterling to euros and posted it back to Bill. She considered writing a note or a card or something but there was nothing to say, so she just posted the cash.

She then did a bit of shopping for the apartment and purchased two blouses for work. She wore black trousers every day that she washed and dried each night on the radiators. There was a tumble dryer, but she didn't want to run up the bill. The nuns had instilled a terrible fear in her of the electricity bill, so Trinity House was always chilly and damp, with wet clothes hung all over the place, and Bill Sheehan would have had a stroke if she suggested getting a dryer when there was a perfectly good clothes line in the garden.

Sharif, in exasperation one evening, cleared the radiators of damp clothes and stuffed everything in the dryer, telling her she was making her asthma worse by having excessive moisture in the air and explaining that he couldn't care less about the electricity bill.

Later, as they sat cuddled up on the sofa watching *Planet Earth 2* by David Attenborough on the huge flat-screen TV, Sharif casually mentioned that his mother was coming back in two days' time. Carmel sat up straight, releasing herself from the comfort of his arms.

'Why didn't you say?' she asked.

'I'm saying it now. What's the problem? She's looking forward to meeting you.' He tried to draw her back into his embrace.

'But you probably haven't told her the full story, that I have a husband back in Ireland that I deserted, that I was in care all my life, that I haven't a bean to my name, that I'm living here gratis and that I'm the wrong side of forty...' Carmel was really getting worked up. Everyone said how close Nadia and Sharif were, and she was sure the older woman would want better for her only child.

Sharif zapped the TV with the remote and the room went quiet. He sat up and faced Carmel. 'Why are you getting so upset? Seriously? Why? She is my mother. I love her and she loves me. All we want for each other is happiness. When my father died, I thought she would fall apart. She might have if it hadn't been for Dolly. Dolly came to our house every day, made my mother get up, wash, dress, do her hair and make-up, and they walked. Miles and miles and miles every day. Sometimes they talked about him, sometimes it was general chat, other times total silence. Dolly knew what she needed. She made her eat, even poured a glass or two of wine down her neck despite my mother being a teetotaller. At least she was then – now she loves a social drink. Seeing how Dolly managed her life alone made my mother realise she could do it too. It broke *Ammi's* heart when Dolly died. As bad if not worse than the loss of my father. She had wanted so much for Dolly to find you. Over the years, my parents threw a lot of resources into tracking you down – by then they were wealthy – but with no success. She knew I was going to Dublin to meet you, but she had to leave for Pakistan to attend my cousin's wedding in Karachi. Otherwise she would have gone to Dublin with me. Her sister's only daughter was the bride so she felt she had to go, but she wished me well and demanded daily updates. The idea that we might feel something for each other never occurred to me, and I hate talking on the phone to her over there as the line is always terrible, so I haven't told her about us. That's a conversation for when I see her face to face. But she will be happy – I know she will. She will see that I love you and that you love me, and that will be all that she will need.'

Carmel paled. Sharif had said he loved her. He'd never said that to her before, and she had never said it to him. Actually, she had never said those words to anyone.

He blushed slightly and gave a small lopsided smile. 'You do love me, don't you?' When her eyes filled with tears, he was instantly apologetic. 'I'm so sorry. I shouldn't have rushed you. It's only been a few weeks, and it's been such an upheaval for you. I'm sorry, Carmel. Forget I said anything...'

She shook her head, not trusting herself to speak.

'What? No, you don't? No, you do?' Sharif was confused.

'I do...love you, I mean. So much it terrifies me, to be honest. I just never heard those words before, never, from anyone. I've never heard them, nor have I ever said them. I...' She was too choked up to speak.

Sharif gathered her to his chest and held her tightly. 'My darling girl, I love you so much and I always will. I want to try to fill that place in your poor battered heart. It's all over now, I swear to you. The misery is over. It's all good from here on. You have my word. I love you so much, and I will take care of you. We'll take care of each other. This is your happy ever after.'

That night she cried in his arms and he didn't try to stop her or try to place any demands on her. He just held her and let her drain herself of all the pain, the pent-up emotion, suppressed for so long. She cried until she felt she had no more tears left in her, and then, as the sun rose, he made her a cup of tea and wrapped her in a blanket and together they watched the sunrise in their little courtyard.

The next day, Sharif insisted she take a day off, so when he left to go on his rounds, she crawled back into their bed and slept for eight hours straight. She woke, washed her hair and dressed. Sharif wasn't there and she wondered where he was, but for the first time there was no panic that he'd come to his senses and left her. He was probably at his own apartment, a place he'd not slept in since she got there but where his clothes and belongings still were.

She texted him. *Hello. I finally woke – I slept all day. Hope your day went well.* She paused, willing her fingers to type the words. She steadied herself and did it. *I love you, Sharif. C xx*

She pressed send and tried to remain calm. He would not think she was a needy, pathetic woman. He'd said he loved her. He was an honest man.

I love you more. I'll be there shortly, will bring some food. S xxxx

CHAPTER 24

Two days later, after spending a huge amount of money in the local Waitrose, Carmel was cooking a welcome dinner for Nadia in her very own kitchen. Sharif had said he was happy to take them both out for dinner, but Carmel wanted to cook and hopefully make a good impression. Mothers liked their sons to be with women who could take care of them surely?

She decided to cook something Irish, mainly because she had no clue what went into Pakistani dishes. The food tasted delicious whenever Sharif cooked, but it was so exotic, she was sure she'd mess it up. She checked and double-checked that Nadia wasn't allergic to anything, and she made home-made cream of vegetable soup from scratch with a freshly baked loaf of soda bread to start, followed by roast lamb with all the trimmings, stuffing, gravy, mashed and roast spuds, carrots and parsnips creamed together and steamed broccoli. For dessert, she was just putting the finishing touches on an apple sponge cake that she was going to serve with custard. Sharif mentioned that his mother enjoyed a glass of white wine now, after a lifetime of sobriety, so Carmel had bought an expensive bottle; she had no idea what it would taste like, as she'd only ever had wine herself a few times with Sharif. Bill used to go down to Seano's pub for a pint three nights a week, but he never invited her, and she never went to social occasions where the possibility of having a drink would present itself.

She got the meat from the halal butcher on the high street, even though Sharif assured her that neither he nor his mother was a strict Muslim. He teased her gently about the elaborate preparations but admitted he was touched she was going to so much trouble and, before going off on his rounds, assured her that his mother was as nervous as she was. Nadia was due to arrive at six, and Carmel wanted the place spotless and everything ready by then. Luckily, she had spent her entire life catering for people so it didn't faze her, and she was confident everything would taste nice. She had bought some lilies for the hall table, and they filled the apartment with their lovely fragrance. As she set the table, she felt a thrill of sheer unadulterated glee at preparing her little home for her first guest.

It was ten to six. Sharif had assured her he'd be back in time, but she knew how he got waylaid frequently by patients or their families and was praying he'd make it. She desperately wanted him there when Nadia arrived. The idea of having to make conversation without Sharif to protect her was petrifying. What if Nadia asked about Carmel's family? *Stop it*, she berated herself. She knew Dolly so she knew Carmel couldn't have a family of her own.

At three minutes past six, with still no sign of Sharif, the doorbell rang. Carmel quickly untied her apron and hung it behind the broom closet door, her stomach churning with nerves. She wanted everything to look perfect. She smoothed down her hair and checked her reflection in the big mirror. She looked like a rabbit in the headlights, startled but frozen in terror, but there was nothing she could do about that.

She opened the door to a small female version of Sharif. The same dark, dark eyes that looked like they were ringed in kohl, the same caramel-coloured skin. Nadia had glossy black hair cut in an elegant style that just stopped short of her shoulders. She had a smooth unlined face, and though Carmel knew she must be at least seventy, she certainly didn't look it. She was so polished and glamorous, Carmel felt dowdy and thrown together by comparison.

'Oh my word. I can't believe it. You are the image of your mother, the absolute image.' Nadia beamed with delight as she entered the apartment, all the time gazing at Carmel. 'I'm sorry for staring, my dear – you must think me so rude – but honestly, the resemblance, it's quite remarkable. It's as if Dolly is standing in front of me again, all these years later. She was blond, of course, but other than that, it is uncanny. Oh how she would have loved to have been reunited with you.'

Carmel was a little taken aback by the effusive nature of the greeting, but at least Nadia seemed pleased to meet her. 'Thank you. It's lovely to meet you, Mrs Khan. Sharif has told me a lot about you,' she managed.

'Nadia, please. And I'm sure that he has, like when the old battleaxe is coming back!' She laughed, the same earthy chuckle as her son. Carmel knew instinctively Nadia was a person she would like, but Nadia had yet to learn the nature of the relationship between her and Sharif. Would she be so pleased then, Carmel wondered.

'Now!' Nadia clapped her hands. A series of gold rings glistened on her fingers, and on her delicate wrist were several jewelled bangles. 'Let's sit down and have a chat before my son comes back, get to know each other a little?' She proffered a gift bag containing two bottles of champagne and an elaborately wrapped box of chocolates.

'Thanks,' Carmel said, accepting the gift and placing one bottle in the ice bucket. 'I mean, thank you very much. You shouldn't have.' She had never entertained anyone before and prayed she wasn't making a total mess of it.

'Not at all, just a small thing.' Nadia dismissed the gift with a wave of her hand. 'I got it in duty-free. Such a gruelling flight from Karachi. We had a three-hour layover in Charles de Gaulle, a wretched place, so I had nothing to do but shop for a few hours. It dragged, as I was so excited to get home and see you. Sharif told me in a text that you looked like her, but honestly, I can't stop staring. I must dig out some of the old photos of her at your age – you'll be astounded.'

Unlike Sharif, who sounded completely English, Nadia had a strong Pakistani accent despite many years living in the UK.

'There's one of her and my late husband, Khalid. We were at a festival or something, and it could be you if you had blond hair. Oh, how he loved your mother! They would laugh for hours. She delighted him, as she did all of us. Even in his last days – and I was only able to keep him at home because of your mother, she helped with everything – she could make him chuckle and forget the pain for a moment at least.' Nadia looked wistful then, as the pain of his loss shadowed her face for a second. 'But listen to me blathering on. I'm nervous, you see, of meeting you, and when I'm nervous, I babble. Tell me all about you.' She patted the seat beside her, and Carmel reluctantly sat down. She hated being in the spotlight of anyone's attention – she was more of a background person – but Nadia was insistent.

Nadia's eyes were so dark it was almost impossible to distinguish between the iris and the pupil, and she had Sharif's long curling lashes. It was clear who he took after, though his father must have been a tall man because Sharif was almost six feet and Nadia barely five.

'Well, there's nothing much to tell really,' she began.

'Oh, that accent! So lyrical and musical, I always think. Dolly sounded the exact same way from the time I first met her to the day she left us.'

'I saw a video of her, on Sharif's phone, of her birthday. She had a strong Dublin accent all right,' Carmel agreed, though she thought her own intonation wasn't as strong as her mother's. But then to foreigners all Irish people probably sounded the same.

'And how did you feel, watching it?' Nadia asked her. She was so direct and open, it could have been disconcerting, but her warmth softened it.

'Er...well, he didn't show it to me at first. He gave me her letters to read and these...' She touched the earrings and necklace she hadn't taken off since Sharif had given them to her.

'Ah yes, and how lovely they are on you. She bought them at a place in Karachi, you know? She visited there with Khalid and me and

Sharif – of course, he was just a boy then – for a family occasion. It was after she'd come back from Ireland, and well, it was a very hard time. She tried to fight them in the courts but failed. I never saw her so low, so Khalid suggested we take her to Pakistan. It was such a culture shock for her, but she was all agog at the sights and sounds of Pakistan. She never really went anywhere, you see, apart from here and back to Ireland to try to find you. Have you travelled much?'

'Never. The first time I was out of Ireland was when I came here a few weeks back,' Carmel admitted. There was no point in pretending she was anything other than what she was. If she was to be a permanent fixture in Sharif's life, then Nadia might as well know the unvarnished truth.

Compassion gleamed from Nadia's eyes. 'Did you have a happy life? Were you loved? Sharif said it was not as we thought but didn't go into any details.'

Carmel inhaled. 'It was OK. I was never adopted, even though they told my mother I had been. I don't know why they would have done that. So I lived in a children's home run by nuns, and it was fine. They weren't mean to us, and I wasn't ever…well…you know… It was OK. To answer your question, though, no, I wasn't loved. I was just there. I had a friend, Kit, and we loved each other, but she went to Australia and was killed in a car accident.'

Tears shone in Nadia's eyes, and Carmel wondered if she should have made it sound a bit better.

'Oh, Carmel, I'm so sorry. We tried so hard, honestly. I swear to you on my best friend's memory, we tried everything. At one stage, Khalid employed a private investigator, but the Church authorities over there were like clams. They would reveal nothing. Dolly used to say, "At least some well-to-do family has her. Only the wealthy can afford to adopt, and the Church knows how to turn a few bob." And after each failed attempt, she would retreat to her little flat and we wouldn't see her for days. I learned that she just needed to be alone and I didn't bother her, and then she would re-emerge, ready to try again. I remember on one occasion, we were all on holiday together, Spain or the Canary Islands or someplace – it doesn't matter anyway.

Sharif was with us. Anyway he wanted to go to an aquarium, so we went. There was one of those places where you walk underneath a glass tunnel and the fish all swim above you – you know the thing I mean?'

Carmel nodded; she'd seen them on TV.

'Well, there was an old shark there, all cuts and scrapes and scars. I don't know how it got there, but it was wild at some point. And Dolly looked at him, with his bright black eye just on the other side of the glass, and she said to me, "That's me, Nad, battered and bruised, but I'll keep on swimming."

'As we walked back to the car park that day – Khalid was up ahead with Sharif – she asked me, "Do you think I'll ever find her? Really?"

'We were always honest with each other, and Khalid was convinced there was nowhere else to look. I didn't want to be negative, but I felt I owed her the truth. I told her that I thought the chances were slim but that miracles do happen. And now here you are.'

'Too late,' Carmel said ruefully.

'For her, yes, but not for you. Now what happened after you left the home?' Nadia paused and seemed to reconsider. 'I'm sorry, am I being too intrusive? We are all total strangers to you, though we feel like we know you. Tell me to mind my own business if you want to.'

Carmel smiled. Nobody had ever asked her anything about her life before Sharif appeared. It was a little disconcerting, she had to admit, but these people loved her mother and their questions came from concern, not nosiness. 'I got married.' She had no idea how to proceed with this. The past was one thing, but this was the very real present, and she had a living, breathing husband in Ireland. Sharif had said his mother wasn't particularly religious, but even so, she might be horrified.

'And was it a good marriage?'

'No. No, it wasn't. He wanted a cook and a cleaner and a maid to take care of his daughters. We weren't in love – I don't think he even liked me much, to be honest. And his sister made sure I never bonded with the little girls. I left him.' Carmel exhaled. At least that part was over with.

'Good for you! You deserve so much more than that. How long ago did you split up?'

'Almost four weeks ago. I left when Sharif found me.'

Both women turned then to the sound of Sharif's key in the lock.

Nadia leapt up and ran to greet him, throwing her arms around him. 'Ah, *mere laal*! My darling boy, how wonderful to see you again!'

'Hello, *Ammi*. So you survived Karachi? You look well.' He grinned, returning her embrace. 'I see you two have met. I'm so sorry I'm late back, Carmel. I was talking to a patient.'

'That's no problem,' she replied, glad to get to the kitchen to make sure her meticulously prepared dinner wasn't burned and to be out from under the spotlight of Nadia's attention.

Sharif led his mother to the lounge area and, taking the bottle from the ice bucket where Carmel had put it, poured three glasses of champagne. 'Carmel, come here when you're ready. I want to propose a toast,' he called as she covered the meat in tinfoil and laid it on the worktop to allow it to rest before carving. Everything else was being kept warm.

She wondered as she crossed the room if she should stand beside him or not and decided against it, thinking it might be too presumptuous. He took the decision out of her hands when he casually slung his arm around her shoulder and kissed her on the lips.

'Oh my goodness! Am I imagining things? Are you two an item, as they say?' Nadia's eyes were wide with surprise.

'Yes, *Ammi*. I love her, and she seems to love me too, though why, I can't imagine.' Sharif chuckled and gave Carmel a squeeze.

'But you never said! In your text you told me you'd found her, but you never mentioned a romance...'

'*Ammi*! That's not news for a text – you know that. You've been trying to pair me off for years, and now your wish will come true.' He winked at Carmel, who tried to smile but she was still worried about Nadia's reaction.

If Nadia wasn't happy about it, then it couldn't work; she knew how close they were. Suddenly, she found herself enveloped in a fragrant hug.

'Oh, Carmel, this is wonderful news! I am so happy for you both. I knew there was something different about him – he seemed to be glowing – but I could never have guessed... Oh, this is just splendid. My son has been alone for too long. And you, Carmel, if anyone deserves a bit of happiness, it is you, my dear. Oh, if only Khalid and Dolly could see this, it would be...' She couldn't go on.

'It's OK, *Ammi.*' Sharif kissed his mother's head, his arms around both women. 'It's OK. This is how it was meant to be.'

CHAPTER 25

*W*ith relief, Carmel pushed the new SIM card into the slot on her phone. A new life, a new number – now nobody from Ireland could contact her. She punched in numbers to her contacts list from the notebook on her desk, a list longer than she could ever have imagined possible before. Various teachers and group activity leaders, some patients' family numbers, Sharif's, of course, and Nadia's, and all the staff members, many of whom she now called friends. Her old phone had had four contacts: Bill, Niamh, Sinead and Julia. She'd had no life in Ballyshanley; the longer she was away, the more obvious it became. Here, she was someone people sought out, texted to see if she wanted to have coffee, someone who got texts from their partner just to say hi. Nobody seemed to see her as poor Carmel. Nobody pitied her or looked down on her. She was a colleague, a girlfriend, a friend, and she absolutely loved it.

She was invited to the cinema to see a film with Ivanka, Ivy, Marlena and Nadia on Friday night and for a pizza afterwards. For them, it was just a regular girls' night, as they called it, but it was the first time she'd ever socialised with a group of friends. She was so excited but tried to be as nonchalant as they were.

The first Sunday she was in London, she got up and prepared for

Mass as she had done every Sunday for forty years. Sharif barely stirred because he'd been up most of the night with a patient who was in distress. As she was about to go out the door, she caught a glimpse of herself in the mirror and a sudden realisation hit her. She didn't have to go.

So, she decided, there and then, that she wouldn't go any more. She instantly started to panic, thinking something awful could happen, but she resisted the urge to run down to the church. Instead, she went for a walk around the grounds, down past the manicured flower beds and lawns, around the polytunnels where the residents grew vegetables for the restaurant, up past the little lake stocked with huge gold koi. On the other side of the lake was the chapel of rest. It was away from the main area of the clinic and was landscaped with trees and shrubs. It wasn't dedicated to any faith group, and so anyone who wished to could be laid out there when they died, and their families could spend some time with their remains. She'd never been in such a place before and was a little nervous. She remembered Julia refusing to go to the funeral of a neighbour because he was a Protestant and she would not go inside the door of a Protestant church. Taking a deep breath and dispelling all thoughts of her hatchet-faced sister-in-law, Carmel pushed the large oak door and stepped inside. The interior felt cool and calm, with its gold carpeting and midnight-blue upholstered seats. It felt like a spiritual place but without the crucifixes or statues. There were fresh flowers and some soothing pieces of art on the walls.

She knelt, even though there were no kneelers. Instead of pews, there were individual seats. She blessed herself as she'd done every day of her life. She began to rattle out the prayers drilled into her as a child; then she stopped. Like Mass, they were meaningless. She sat down and breathed deeply, feeling what she wanted to say in her heart before uttering it.

'Hi, Mam.' She spoke quietly, though she was alone. 'I've never called you that. I suppose nobody else ever did either. I wish I could have met you. I wish we could have been together. But you wanted me, I know that now, and Sharif and Nadia have been so kind. They talk about you all the time, and I feel like you can see us. I hope you can anyway. I'm so sorry that they never let you come for me. I would have loved it if you could have. I had a lonely life – I only know how lonely it was since I've come here. I hope you're happy now, and I hope...well, I hope you're proud of how I turned out.'

She sat in silence for a long time, just thinking. She took the new photo album out of her bag and opened it once more. Nadia had given her lots more pictures, taken at various points in Dolly's life, and presented them to her in a beautiful album covered in cream lace and with Dolly's name embroidered on the front. Sharif revealed that Nadia had made the album herself. Carmel treasured it.

The only photos of Dolly's life before coming to England were the one of Carmel as a baby and the one taken on Dollymount Strand that just said 'Me and Joe, Dollymount, 1973.' It had been taken by a professional photographer and bore the name of a photographic studio long gone from Clontarf Road, opposite the beach. She'd googled it to see if any trace of it might still exist, but those days when photographers took pictures of couples and they paid a few shillings and collected the snap later were long gone. Everyone had smartphones now.

Why would she have included that one, Carmel wondered? Was Joe her father? And if so, Joe who? She tried to see any resemblance between herself and the man in the picture but failed. Everyone who knew Dolly was astounded at the resemblance between her and Carmel, so she wondered if she had any of her father in her at all.

Joe could have been a brother, or a friend, or an old boyfriend. The body language between the couple in the photo was certainly relaxed and loving, but beyond that it was hard to say. Carmel was born in 1976 and this photo was taken in 1973. If this smiling young man was her father, then he and Dolly would have been together at least three years, and surely then that relationship would have survived an unplanned pregnancy, even in those days? Dolly wasn't a wimp. She and this Joe, if he was the father, could surely have taken the boat to England together and had Carmel there and lived happily ever after. They both looked very young in the photo, but three years later they'd have been able to fend for themselves even in holy Catholic Ireland.

Neither Nadia nor Sharif could shed any light on who Joe was, or who her father might have been. Apparently, Dolly never mentioned it.

'I asked her once, years ago,' Nadia revealed when they'd discussed it last, 'but she wouldn't say anything except that he was the love of her life and that he was married.'

'Did he know she was pregnant, do you think?' Carmel didn't know what answer she was hoping for. No, probably, because then he wouldn't have knowingly abandoned her.

'I don't know. I'm so sorry, Carmel. I wish I knew more. But for someone so open, she was very, very private about certain things. We were as close as sisters, but we all have some secrets that never leave our own hearts. Dolly's relationship with your father, whatever that was, fell into that category, I'm afraid.'

Carmel sat in the church for a while, just breathing, thinking about her mother, and a sense of calm settled over her. She thought of the nuns who raised her, most of them dead now too, of Kit, and she had a little word with each of them. She prayed, not in the rote way she'd been taught, but in her own way, using her own words. She enjoyed the solitude and the connection with something beyond herself far more than she'd ever done in St Augustine's church in Ballyshanley, with Julia's shrill voice drowning out the choir and Father Linehan's droning that used identical intonation for each sentence.

She let herself back into the apartment to discover Sharif had gone to check on a patient. They were going out to lunch with a doctor friend of his and his wife, and she was dreading it. It was something arranged before Sharif even came over to Ireland. He said he didn't particularly want to go, but they were both involved with some upcoming conference so he kind of had to.

He thought she might enjoy meeting the doctor's wife. Sometimes she thought Sharif was totally oblivious to the clear differences between them, but the rest of the world was not. A couple of the less pleasant patients had made catty remarks about her having herself well and truly ensconced in a very lucrative set-up, and when she accidentally overheard them, her face burned with shame. They were right, of course, but what they didn't know was that she would love Sharif Khan if he were unemployed and penniless. She cared nothing for money, and funnily enough, despite the fact that he was very wealthy, neither did Sharif.

He believed completely in the idea that prosperity came easily to those who tried to do good with the money they accrued. His primary focus was providing a comfortable home for those at the last phase of their lives and making their deaths as positive and as peaceful an experience as it could be. It was expensive, no doubt about it, but Sharif had explained that the vast majority of people had money by the time their lives were ending. They owned houses and so on to sell, so they could enjoy some comfort after their years of hard work. Most families would rather see their loved ones well taken care of and happy in their final days, weeks or months than have an extra few thousand in their inheritance. Carmel suspected several of the residents of Aashna were either there on a heavily subsidised basis or free of charge altogether – she'd spoken to many who came from backgrounds that would not have supported the fees Aashna charged – but Sharif never commented on that.

She had some time to get ready anyway for the lunch; that was something. She was going to need some major refurbishment to make herself presentable enough to his friends. People at Aashna were one thing – they were so welcoming, and the fact that she was 'baby Carmel' certainly oiled the wheels – but a fancy doctor and his wife in a posh restaurant was something entirely different.

CHAPTER 26

*C*armel had spent what she considered an astronomical amount of money on a dress in Marks & Spencer at the insistence of Ivanka and Zane, who spotted it as they walked through the store on their way to a pub they sometimes went to for lunch. She had tried to take a much bigger size into the changing room, but Zane and Ivanka hooted with laughter. She couldn't believe it when the size ten dress fitted her perfectly; all the lumps and bumps caused by years of comfort eating seemed to have melted away. She knew Sharif liked her when they met in Dublin, but she must have seemed so frumpy to him then. At least now she looked much better, even if her insecurities were still there.

The dress was royal blue and very figure-hugging, not her usual sort of thing at all, with sheer sleeves and a skirt that stopped just above the knee. Its round neck was encrusted with tiny silver sequins. It looked very glamorous in the shop, but Carmel felt ridiculous in it. She also bought a pair of impossibly high silver strappy sandals, under considerable pressure from Zane, that she was sure would result in a trip to the emergency department, but he assured her that beauty was pain and that she looked fabulous.

Carmel had never met anyone like Zane in her life. He was very animated and theatrical, and she only understood about half of what he said, speaking as he did in a hybrid of cockney rhyming slang and some kind of American rap. He told her that he stayed fit by doing Zumba, and when she asked what it was, proceeded to give her a demonstration of some very suggestive dancing in the middle of the supermarket. He'd found her embarrassment hilarious. At the checkout ten minutes later, a youngish man in a business suit started joking around with them, complimenting Zane on his dancing. Carmel would have tried to get away – men who started conversations in the supermarket with strangers were best avoided – but Zane revelled in the attention, flirting outrageously. They ended up exchanging numbers.

Carmel was shocked at how open he was, and over coffee she managed to get up the courage to ask him about his life.

'It's mostly harmless.' He shrugged, then sipped a confection called a Coco Loco Frappuccino.

'So you don't go out with all the men you meet?' Carmel asked, fascinated.

'No, of course I don't!' he squealed. 'What do you think I am? No, Carmel, I'm not after a "roll in the hay" as you might say over in Ireland.'

She didn't bother to disavow him of the idea; nobody in Ballyshanley would ever say such a thing. She sometimes thought Zane mixed Ireland and the Wild West of America up.

'I'm looking for love.' Suddenly all the dramatics were gone and he was sincere and vulnerable.

'And is that easy to find?' she asked innocently.

'What do you reckon?' He arched one perfectly waxed eyebrow.

'Well, it took me forty years,' Carmel conceded.

'Exactly, mate.' He nodded sagely.

'Who is your ideal partner then?' She knew she was prying, but Zane was so open that he wouldn't mind.

He thought for a moment. 'Someone my dad would accept,' he said sadly.

Carmel had never seen Zane in any mode but outrageously flamboyant, so this was new. 'And what kind of a guy would that be?' She was intrigued.

Zane sighed and drained his creamy frozen coffee, the straw gurgling loudly. 'The kind that's a girl.'

'Oh.' Carmel didn't really know what to say. 'Doesn't he know you're gay?' For a terrible moment she thought he might cry.

'He knows, but he won't talk to me, not really. He talks to me through my mum, like he's afraid to have any direct connection in case he catches it off me or something. I've tried, but he's not having it. He's Jamaican, a big Black dude, and he's embarrassed by me.' The pain was there to hear. 'Reckons there wasn't ever a gay man in the family, blames my mum's side. When I was little, he was great, you know, took me playing football, taught me to ride a bike, to swim, all that stuff, but since I came out, nothing.'

'I'm sorry, Zane. That's so hard.'

He shrugged. 'That's life, though, ain't it?'

Ivanka knocked on the door and arrived with a large vanity case. She had promised to come round to do Carmel's hair and make-up before the lunch, and true to her word spent the next forty minutes applying all sorts of potions and lotions to Carmel's skin and then blow-drying her hair until it was sleek and glossy before using what felt like an inordinate number of pins and grips to make her hair do what Ivanka wanted it to do.

When Carmel finally looked in the full-length mirror in their bedroom, she had to admit the transformation was remarkable. Her hair was twisted into an elegant up style and pinned with little sparkly clips that caught the light when she turned her head. She'd gone for a trim to the hairdresser's the week before, and the very camp man who ran the place screamed in horror at the brown dye in her hair, insisting he strip it all out and restore her to her natural colour. He was so determined that she let him, and anyway she hated the brown – it reminded her of that old crow Julia. And so four hours and 160 pounds later, she emerged, blond once more. Sharif got a fright when he saw her, but he assured her that he loved it and that now her face made more sense. They'd giggled at his description, but she knew what he meant. Her creamy skin and blue eyes worked so much better with her natural honey blond than with the mousy-brown colour. She'd spent more money on herself in the last month than she'd ever done in her entire life, nudged along by Ivanka and Zane, who had really taken her under their wing.

Zane thought nothing of standing outside changing rooms in women's clothes shops, giving a hilarious running commentary on her new wardrobe. She looked nothing like her former self, and she'd even upgraded her work uniform from a selection of pastel blouses and black trousers to skirts, tops and even jackets. She still loved her jeans and T-shirts when lounging around, but Sharif always looked so elegant; she felt less like a scarecrow beside him when she dressed up a bit.

'So.' Ivanka stood back, admiring her handiwork. 'You now look beautiful.'

Ivanka looked intimidating, with her arctic-blue eyes that slanted beautifully, her perfect straight nose and gleaming white teeth, but beneath the icy exterior beat a heart of gold. She was gentle with patients and worked hard to alleviate as much suffering as she could.

'I don't know about beautiful, but certainly better anyway. I used to look like someone covered me in glue and threw me into a charity shop.' Carmel smiled at her friend. 'Thanks, Ivanka.'

Her phone beeped. *Hi, darling. I had to take a patient to Bedford for emergency surgery, so I won't get back in time to pick you up. Would you mind taking a taxi to the restaurant and I'll meet you there? S x*

Darling. The idea of Bill calling her darling, or anything except Carmel, made her smile, but Sharif was naturally expressive and it didn't sound odd coming from him.

She would have preferred to arrive with him for moral support, but she was a big girl now, she told herself. She could do this.

She ordered the cab to pick her up at reception and got several appreciative comments and even a wolf whistle from Kate as she passed, which made her blush. Kate and Sheila were installing one of their bird feeders outside reception.

The restaurant was so posh it could hurt itself, as Kit used to say. It was an old country mansion, all banisters and glittering candelabras and chandeliers. A doorman, in full regalia, held the door open for her. 'Good afternoon, madam. Welcome to Grosslyn Court.'

What on earth was she doing here? The urge to bolt threatened to overwhelm her as she stood in the vast entrance hall. Waiting staff flurried about, carrying impossibly heavy silver platters and serving dishes. There appeared to be dining rooms on either side of the grand staircase. She had no idea what to do next. Should she try one of the rooms to see if Sharif was there? Or call him maybe? Perhaps people didn't just whip out mobile phones in places like this. Though she thought she looked OK, inside she felt like little Carmel Murphy, nobody's child and completely out of place in such opulent surroundings. She debated going back outside, maybe wait for Sharif there, but as she deliberated, trying not to get in anyone's way, she spotted him emerging from a taxi. Relief flooded through her; it was going to be fine. She smiled and went to meet him, but he didn't see her. He turned to enter the dining room on the left. When she put her hand on his arm, he spun around and gazed in amazement. 'Carmel...I didn't recognise you! You look... Oh my God, you look absolutely beautiful. That dress, and your hair... I had no idea it was you.'

She beamed with delight. 'Ivanka did it, really. She and Zane made me buy the dress, even though it cost ninety-five pounds!' she whispered in his ear.

He grinned. 'You crack me up. Honestly, you do. The women in here would spend that on a lipstick, and not one of them could hold a candle to you. I'm the luckiest man alive. Now let's take you in so I can show you off to Tristan and Angelica.'

She picked her way behind him to a table where a couple sat waiting in silence. As they rose to greet Sharif and Carmel, Carmel sensed a coldness in the embrace, especially from Angelica. They were both very rich looking, expensive clothes and shoes, but Angelica was polished and perfect and Tristan definitely was not. He had that high-bred look about him, all ruddy cheeks and sticking-out ears. His reddish hair was receding, but he had it strategically styled in a not-very-convincing comb-over, and his voice was nasal and reed thin. She was totally different, all shiny black hair cut in a severe bob, heavy make-up and scarlet-red lips. Her dress was a little too tight, and Carmel suspected it was cutting her in half. A lifetime spent in the shadows meant Carmel was good at spotting the things more extroverted people missed, and the tension between this pair was palpable.

Tristan was an oncologist as well, and he and Sharif immediately began discussing another colleague's upcoming article in *The Lancet*, leaving her in the full beam of Angelica's inquisitive stare.

'So, Carmel, you're Irish, I understand?' Angelica raised an impeccably plucked black eyebrow. She might as well have said, 'I hear you're a leper,' for all the warmth in her voice.

'Yes, Dublin originally, and later County Offaly.' Carmel tried to sound confident but feared she failed miserably.

'I've never been. Tristan went once, hunting or fishing or something mind-numbing like that, but I've never felt the urge. It's terribly green, I believe.' Her accent could have cut glass.

'Eh, yes, very green all right. In fact, Johnny Cash wrote a song about Ireland called "Forty Shades of Green",' Carmel blurted, feeling instantly imbecilic.

'Johnny who? Do we know him? Sharif used to know a chap, years ago, second trombone or some such, with the Berlin Philharmonic?' She looked perplexed.

Oh, God, Carmel thought, did she have to take this conversation to its mortifying conclusion? 'No, he's an American country singer – well, was. He's dead now.' Carmel could feel the colour creeping up her neck. She took a big gulp of water.

'An American?' Angelica wrinkled her nose. 'Oh, no, I don't know many of those. My father knew some – they were stationed at our country house during the war or something, back when he was a child – but I tend to avoid Americans where possible. Though it is becoming increasingly more difficult.' She uttered this broad, racist generalisation and dabbed her lips with the starched napkin, leaving a blood-red stain that someone was going to have to scrub to remove.

Sharif and Tristan were still deep in conversation, so escape looked unlikely.

'I'd love to visit there someday,' Carmel ventured, trying to defend all the Americans she loved to listen to on podcasts and on TED Talks.

'Well, why on earth would you not go if that is your wish?' Angelica fixed Carmel with an icy gaze as if she were a particularly slow five-year-old.

'Well, it would cost a lot, flights and all of that. I'd have to save up.' Carmel wasn't going to try to keep up with her; it would be impossible anyway.

'Quite.'

Carmel could tell she wasn't sure if it was a joke.

The huge leather-bound menus arrived, and to Carmel's dismay, the menu was written almost entirely in what she thought might be French. She didn't do French at school; it was only needed if you were going to college, so she did geography instead. Kids in state care were never considered as university material. It was never said outright, but the inference was that she had cost the state quite enough already without expecting a third-level qualification as well.

She tried to make out what the words on the menu might mean. Sometimes French words looked a bit like English words she'd heard. But even the bits that were in English were a mystery. The whole thing was *confits* of this and *veloutés* of that. She imagined sweetbreads to be a dessert of some kind, but they were being served with samphire, whatever that was, and potato rosti. The only thing she recognised was potato, and that couldn't be a dessert, could it? Sharif must have noticed her discomfort and asked if he should order for her.

'Yes, please, that would be lovely. I'm just going to the ladies. You know what I like.' She dared to rest her hand on his shoulder as she passed, and he reached up and covered it with his, holding her gaze for a second. She walked away, happy that he loved her even if she didn't fit in with these surroundings or these people.

When she returned, Angelica was halfway through a bottle of

white wine and Sharif had barely touched his glass of red. Tristan was driving so was only drinking mineral water. Angelica smiled, but Carmel thought she looked like a particularly hungry fox.

'So you found it all right? This place is a bit of a maze. I used to come here as a teenager, when the Wesley-Cramptons had it. Old Charlie W.C., as everyone called him, was a frightful goat – one had to keep one's wits about them if he was on the prowl – but the parties were marvellous. One occasion, I recall Grahame Billingsley – do you know him? Top man at London Bridge Hospital – Sharif knows him. Anyway, he was caught *in flagrante* as it were with Georgia Samsworth's au pair. Georgia went totally berserk, and we all thought she was outraged that he should take advantage of such a girl. But no, it turns out that she herself was involved with Grahame for years and nobody knew. The same night, Grahame's wife was there, as was Georgia's current husband, Danny Porchion-Wall. They divorced, but her father was a QC – now sits on the appellate bench – so she got everything.'

Carmel looked at Angelica in bewilderment, but the other woman ploughed on regardless. Carmel had absolutely no idea what she was going on about. At least Angelica required no input from Carmel. She droned on for several minutes, name-dropping double barrels here and there, and everyone she knew was the top of something. Carmel looked around and took in the splendour of the room until Sharif's voice broke through her reverie.

'Tristan, we have been derelict in our duties to these beautiful ladies, going on about work. Forgive us – we are boring when we get on the subject of molecular mutations in genome sequencing.'

'One of you is boring no matter what he talks about.' Angelica's derisive remark went unheard by the men but not by Carmel.

The afternoon dragged on, and Sharif soon saw that Carmel wasn't enjoying it. Angelica was getting drunker by the second – she'd ordered another bottle of wine, having polished off the first one single-handedly – and her sneering remarks about her husband were more audible.

Tristan was all right, but he had nothing to say to the women, it would seem. He listened politely whenever Sharif drew Carmel into the conversation, but once she'd finished, he'd raise some totally unrelated topic again with Sharif, inevitably one in which she couldn't participate.

After the main course, where Angelica made a huge deal of how she wanted everything served and then ate none of it, the waiter came offering desserts, but Sharif checked his beeper.

'Oh, I'm sorry, folks, we have to go. I'm needed at Aashna.' He smiled apologetically, but Carmel saw the conspiratorial gleam in his eye.

'Oh, for God's sake, can't the registrar do it?' Angelica whined, her red-taloned hand on Sharif's sleeve. 'We've hardly seen you for months and now you're dashing off. Anybody would think you were trying to get away, but then perhaps you are. After all, there's only so much scientific drivel a person can listen to without wanting to stab a bloody boring talking head with a steak knife.'

Sharif looked at her intently, clearly embarrassed for his friend. 'Perhaps you should cut back on the booze, Angelica. It doesn't agree with you.' Sharif's words were mild but packed a punch all the same.

Angelica reddened with embarrassment. 'Oh, Sharif, don't be such a bore. Come on, stay and have some fun.' She tried to recover, but it only made everyone else at the table cringe.

Tristan shut his eyes in resignation; he was clearly tired of her constant sniping. 'Well, you must get on, old boy. Thanks for coming. I'll be in touch about the call for papers. The conference isn't until the spring, but I'd like to have a strong representation from our end if possible.' He turned his attention to Carmel. 'It was lovely to meet you, Caroline.' He held out his hand to shake hers.

'Carmel, Tristan. Her name is Carmel,' Sharif said gently.

'Of course, of course, what did I call you? Something else? I'm so sorry, my dear. I'm a bit...well, you know.' Tristan at least had the good grace to look embarrassed, but Carmel knew he had no more interest in her than the man in the moon. Sharif was clearly his focus and the ladies were mere decorations.

Tristan's relationship with his wife left a lot to be desired, and while Carmel felt sorry for him in the way Angelica sniped constantly, if she had to play second fiddle to his career and listen to him droning on about molecules or whatever all day, maybe she had some reason to be so catty.

CHAPTER 27

*I*n the cab on the way back to Aashna House, Sharif took her hand. 'I'm sorry. That was a terrible lunch for you, and you looked so stunning... I'm really sorry.'

'Sharif, they're your friends and they seem nice, I suppose. I just don't know the set of people she was on about, the Tingly-Melons or the Fartalots or whatever.'

He laughed and seemed relieved she wasn't angry.

'Honestly, please don't feel upset. It was a lovely lunch. I'd never been anywhere so fancy in all my life, and the food was out of this world. Did you know Angelica used to visit there before it was a hotel, when it was just a private house? Can you imagine?'

Sharif chuckled. 'Don't be fooled by the cut-glass accent. Angelica comes from a long line of social climbers. Her mother was originally a hairdresser and her father a butcher, but they did well, both retiring with huge chains of shops all over London. The ailing and penniless aristocracy are desperate for cash and will marry anyone who has it. Poor old Tristan's father gambled everything they had, so when Angelica showed up and set her cap at him, it seemed the answer to both their prayers. Angelica gets status and a crumbling old pile to call home, and the right honourables get the central heating fixed and patch up the roof with their working-class fortunes. Everyone's a winner, you would think, except that the toffs secretly despise those they need so badly for money and the hairdressers' daughters resent the uselessness of the lords and ladies. It hardly ever works out in practice.'

'And which bracket do you fit into?' she asked with a grin.

'Oh, neither.' He chuckled, then put on a cockney accent. 'I'm just a Paki who done good. Neither group would lower themselves for the likes of me. No, I had to go to the Emerald Isle to find a woman who thankfully wouldn't know the social ladder from one in her stocking, and I love her for it.' He drew her towards him in the back seat of the cab and kissed her.

'Careful, Dr Khan. I might start getting notions of upperosity myself now. A doctor is a serious catch for a girl with nothing and no one to her name. Maybe I'll go for elocution lessons and learn to say "simply marvellous" or "what-ho chaps".' Carmel put on a silly posh accent and Sharif chucked.

'Please don't. I don't ever want you to change, not one single thing. When I was at university, I worked very hard. My mother and father did the same. My father almost worked himself to death when he came here, but he wanted better for me, for my mother. He had corner shops. Cliché, I know, but it was a business a young Pakistani immigrant could get a start in, and if you worked hard enough, you could expand it. People see me now, with Aashna House and all of it, but I'm from very humble people, hard-working people, who knew the value of a pound. Their blood is in my veins. Yes, now I live in luxury, so does my mother, but it wasn't always like this and I care very little for the trappings of wealth. I'm not a member of their clubs nor do I own a boat or a horse. I'm a simple man, with simple needs and desires. When Jamilla died, I never imagined I'd ever feel like that about anyone ever again. I knew her all my life – our parents were friends – and she got it, you know? Her father and mine emigrated together, and we grew up together. Weird as it might sound, she would have loved you. She had no time for that whole social-climbing business either. She got that I didn't want to be a doctor so I could make lots of money. I did it because I really wanted to make a difference to people's lives.' He sounded so sincere, and his dark eyes burned with purpose and honesty.

'I don't fit in with those people, Carmel. Tristan and Angelica and all of them, they just see the clinic and they calculate the money I must be making and decide to befriend me based on that. I normally refuse all those invitations, but I do want to be involved with the conference. There's some cutting-edge stuff up for discussion there, particularly on the use of cannabis for medicinal purposes. Also I'd forgotten what a pain Angelica can be, and I thought it might be nice for you to make some friends, but they're not your type of people either. I'm sorry. I just want you to be happy here. I don't want you to think you made a mistake.'

'Sharif, I have never been so bloody happy in my life. How can you be worried? I love it here. I love Aashna House, England, the patients, the staff, and I especially love that I can feel closer to my mother here. You've saved my life.'

CHAPTER 28

*C*armel's pager buzzed; Marlena was calling her to reception.
The head teacher from the local primary school wanted to
see the events coordinator.

For the first time since Carmel came to Aashna, she felt tired. She
wasn't sleeping. Her mother was on her mind all the time, so many
questions just swirling around her head.

Sharif had taken her to Brighton, to where he and his mother had
scattered Dolly's ashes, and showed her the tree they had planted in
her memory. 'Dolly Mullane, mother and friend, "Que sera, sera"' was
on the inscription. Dolly had asked Sharif to put 'mother' on it in case
Carmel ever found her, which touched Carmel but left her with more
questions to which nobody had answers.

Who was her father? Was he still alive? Would he want to know
her? Why did Dolly feel she had to leave?

The previous night, Carmel barely slept a wink. Eventually getting
up quietly so as not to disturb Sharif, she watched the dawn creep
across the sky as she sipped a cup of tea in the courtyard. Sharif
placing his hand on her shoulder startled her.

'What's up? You haven't slept at all.' He took off his robe, wrapped
it around her and sat down.

She was grateful for the warmth; despite the early summer, it was chilly in the mornings. 'Not really. Just...it's like all the questions I had as a kid have come back to the surface again. But I'm sorry, I shouldn't be keeping you up with all of this. You need to rest. I'm sorry...'

He turned to her. 'Why are you sorry? What for? You have done nothing. Oh, Carmel, my love, I wish I could take some of this burden for you, I really do. And poor Dolly. If only I could have kept her going for another little while, you'd have met her and she would have told you the answers to your questions.'

She smiled and reached for his hand. 'I don't know what I did to deserve you, but I'm so grateful for you being in my life, for you giving me a life, actually.'

'You're saving me too. We're saving each other. Before you, it was just work, work, work. I never socialised or went on holiday – I didn't see the point. Now, with you, everything is different. I'm living and working, not just working.'

Carmel felt proud as she walked down to meet the primary school head teacher and took her to the day room for coffee. The teacher, a large Black lady called Daf, who had a growling infectious laugh, said the children at her school would be putting on a production of, *The Wizard of Oz* once they came back to school after the holidays. She explained that once school resumed in the autumn it was chaotic so she liked to prepare as much as she could for the school play while the school was quiet. It was going to be performed for the parents, but she wondered if the patients would like to see it. The school was just across the road from the clinic and was a very inclusive place by all accounts. There was a posher, fancier school at the other end of town, but this place was a real rainbow of nationalities, religions and ability levels. Sharif always said that if he'd have had children, he'd have sent them there. Just seeing the kids walk by in the mornings and being collected in the afternoons put a smile on lots of the faces of their patients, a reminder that life goes on.

Of course Carmel thought it was a lovely idea and made her first executive decision to go with it. Many patients had visitors but some didn't, and to see the little ones singing and dancing could only bring joy. Daf came alive when she spoke about the kids in her care, and soon the conversation strayed into the more general and some of the difficulties the school faced through lack of funding. Everything was on a shoestring as the parents generally couldn't afford much, and it emerged that the drama team at the school always encountered some trouble sourcing costumes. It was another reason Daf started preparations early, she spent her weeks off scouring charity shops and car boot sales.

Carmel had an idea. 'Maybe we could help you out there? I can sew, and I'm running a sewing circle here in the afternoons. Well, actually, my late mother set it up, so I'm just following in her footsteps.' She smiled inwardly at how she dropped the words 'my mother' into the conversation like a normal person. 'Well, anyway, the patients really love it and they're very good. Maybe if what you needed wasn't that complicated, we could help to run up the costumes? Come to think of it, we also have a Men's Shed thing here. Some of the men enjoy doing woodworking projects. There are patients involved, but local residents, mostly retired, come too every Friday morning. I'm sure if you needed something made for a set, they'd organise that?'

Suddenly, Carmel found herself lost in a sea of dark curly hair as Daf embraced her warmly. 'That would be amazing! Thanks so much! If you're sure it wouldn't be too much? We just need yellow tunic things for the Munchkins, and they can wear black leggings, and if you could make a lot of red belts as well, just a strip of fabric for around the waist. Something like this maybe...' She opened a page on her phone.

'That's easy. I'm sure we can do that. How many do you need?'

Daf winced and said apologetically, 'Would fifty be out of the question? We can buy the material or whatever you need...'

Sharif appeared at her shoulder. 'What's all this? Relaxing over cups of coffee when you're supposed to be working? I don't know, Daf, trying to get good staff these days...' He grinned and kissed Carmel on the cheek, perching on the arm of her chair.

'Hi, Sharif.' Daf turned the spotlight of her beam on him, 'Carmel here is just offering to help with the costumes for the school musical.

160

We're doing *The Wizard of Oz*, and we're going to put on a show here for the patients as well, if that's OK?'

'Of course, thanks for thinking of us. We'll be looking forward to it, I'm sure. Carmel is a dab hand with a needle and thread – she gets it from her mum – and she's got all sorts going on in the sewing class, so I'm sure it will be a great project for them.'

'And I thought the Men's Shed guys could help with the set?'

'Great idea. Between you and me, I think we've quite enough bird feeders, so it'll be good to change focus. The bird feeders are attracting so many birds, my car is covered in droppings every day now!'

Carmel loved his chuckle.

'Well, I was just saying that we'd supply the fabric or whatever they need,' Daf said. 'Our fundraising team has been flat out getting sponsorships. If you can just let me know what lengths or whatever, Carmel...'

'No, not at all. We'll pay for all of that.' Sharif was insistent. 'Let it be our contribution. You just let us know what you want, and we'll take care of it. It's the least we can do if we're getting the West End theatrical experience brought to our very own Aashna House. Hey, maybe we could throw a little party afterwards, you know, for the kids – some sweets, balloons, music, that sort of thing?'

Carmel caught Daf's glance and smiled. Sharif was like a kid himself, and his enthusiasm was infectious.

'The Kaivalya would be perfect. After the performance, we could take out the seats, have a little party. What do you say, ladies?'

Carmel fought the urge to jump up and hug him there and then. He was so emotional, so full of excitement and fun, the very opposite of Bill. 'I think it would be lovely. Daf?'

'Well, I know the kids would love it, but the Kaivalya here is so beautifully decorated and all that glass and the plants and everything – I'm thinking sticky fingers and spilled fruit juice... And as well, wouldn't it be too noisy for the patients? They're a bit hyper at the best of times, but after a performance, they might be very boisterous.'

'No, absolutely not. That's what the Kaivalya was built for. We can clean it up afterwards, no problem. You know what we are like here, Daf – it's not a hushed-tones kind of place. These people are sick, yes, but they're not dead yet, and a bit of fun and craic, as my charming Irish friend might say, would be good for them. Of course, those that don't want to participate don't have to, but nothing lifts the spirits like the smile of a child. It would honestly do everyone here some good. We'd love to host them here and lay on some treats and music or whatever. I'll leave the details to Carmel here. Now, I must go. I'm meeting a new patient.' He kissed Carmel on the head. 'See you later.'

Daf grinned. 'I've known him a long time, and I've never seen him so happy. You two are good together.'

'We are. He's one in a million.'

Daf left, promising to text the details. Carmel made a note on her phone to speak to the sewing circle and the Men's Shed, then made her way back to the main house to check in with the pottery class.

CHAPTER 29

*W*alking through the grounds, Carmel observed the patients, especially the older men, trying to imagine what her father might look like. Dolly was only in her early twenties when Carmel was born, and if her father was this Joe, then he was probably around the same age, which would make him early sixties now. The fact that her mother included the photo of herself and Joe Carmel took to mean that Joe was her father, but maybe not. When Sharif found her in Dublin, he told her what Dolly had told him, that she was young and that Ireland wasn't a kind place for young unmarried girls who found themselves pregnant. So she just assumed the Joe in the photo was her father, but since the trail went cold there, there wasn't any point in further speculation. Dolly had never even told Nadia who Carmel's father was, and Dolly and Nadia were, by all accounts, as close as two friends can be. If they were truly just a young couple in trouble, why the big secret all these years later? In all the letters to Carmel, Dolly never mentioned Joe or any other man, not even once, but then why include the picture?

For the millionth time since she'd arrived at Aashna House, Carmel wished she'd had even one day with her mother, one hour even, just to talk to her, to ask her things. Maybe she would have told her only child who her father was, or maybe not; maybe it was a closed chapter for her.

All was well with the pottery class and Carmel decided to knock off for the evening. She was tired and decided to get an early night. Back in what she always thought of now as their apartment, she made herself a cup of tea and tried to still her racing thoughts.

'A penny for them?' Nadia asked as Carmel gazed out the window.

Carmel spun around; she'd thought she was alone. 'Oh, Nadia, I'm sorry… I wasn't expecting…' She was flustered.

'It's quite all right, my dear. Sharif let me in. I hope you don't mind? He's outside talking to somebody. I was passing and thought I hadn't seen you for a few days. Sharif said you seemed a little distracted. He wasn't telling tales, my dear – he just was worried about you.'

'Oh, I was just thinking about my mother, my father, you know.' She smiled and turned to Nadia.

'Do you feel like a walk?' Something in Nadia's tone suggested it wasn't just a stroll in the evening air that was on offer; she gazed intently at Carmel.

'Sure, OK.'

It was a mild enough evening that she didn't need a coat, and she and Nadia waved a cheery goodbye to Sharif, who was still deep in conversation with one of the physiotherapists.

'We're just going for a walk,' his mother called, and led Carmel away from the clinic, towards the exit of the campus. 'You don't have to tell me anything, Carmel. There were things your mother never revealed to me, and you know how close we were. I understand you may want to keep it to yourself. Every woman has her secrets, but it might help to talk.' Nadia didn't look at her but kept clipping along at a pace that belied her short legs.

Carmel didn't say anything. She'd never had anyone to confide in before, so it didn't come naturally to her.

Nadia chatted on. 'Your mother and I shared everything, even Sharif really. She so longed to have you back, and that void hurt her every day of her life. She and Sharif…' Nadia sighed. 'I will be honest

– sometimes I was jealous of their bond. When he was a teenager, if he had a problem, it was Dolly he would turn to and it hurt me. But she always directed him to me. Always she would say that he should talk to me. And Khalid as well – he loved her too.'

Carmel stopped and looked at the other woman in dismay.

'No, not like that, not in a devious way. He was never unfaithful to me in any way, but he loved Dolly and she loved him. She was like a sister, as I said, but there were things she kept from me. In the last year or two before she died, she would go to visit someone and stay overnight, maybe once or twice a week, and she never said who or why.'

'And you never asked?' Carmel was fascinated.

'No. She knew that I knew and she never volunteered the information, so I never asked. It might sound odd, but we respected each other's privacy. Khalid was gone, Sharif was busy with Aashna, and Dolly had this other life that I knew nothing about. It was hard not to pry, but I loved her too much for that. If she wanted to tell me, she would have, and she didn't.'

Carmel squeezed her arm as they walked. Nadia was so honest, so warm and open. Sharif was wonderful too, and so understanding. But Carmel needed her mother. She'd never needed her as much when she was a child or a new bride or anything like that, but now that she could picture her as a real person, she desperately wanted her guidance. It was all so confusing; she just didn't know how to process it.

'Anyway, enough about me. What has you awake at night?'

'Oh, Nadia, I don't know where to even start...' Carmel heard the despair in her own voice.

'The beginning is usually a good place.' Nadia smiled gently.

'I know I should be so happy,' she began tentatively. It felt so wrong to complain, especially after all Sharif had done for her, but she needed to figure this out. 'And I am, I really am. It's like a dream come true to finally know she was here, she lived, she was real, and she was looking for me, but I just miss her. Like, it's stupid. How can you miss someone you never met? And then I think about my father, and I need to know. I keep thinking I'm seeing him in the street or on the bus. It's ridiculous, I know. Even if he's alive, he's probably in Ireland. And this Joe in the picture… Why did Dolly give me that if he's not my father? I just want to know! When I was little, I used to make up stories in my head about my mammy and daddy, but once I got old enough to realise they weren't going to come for me, I forced it out of my mind. I didn't just forget about them. It was different. I wouldn't allow those thoughts in. But now that I'm here and she's real, I can't stop thinking, wondering. I never had anyone of my own, except Kit, and I should be down on my knees in gratitude for Sharif and you and all of this, but it's like something has woken in me and I can't let it go. I'm going out of my mind, Nadia.'

On they walked.

'I understand, Carmel. It's so much to take in, and of course you numbed it as a child. What else could you do? And all those years with that man, Bill, well, that was so hard for you too. But shall I tell you something I've discovered?'

Carmel nodded.

Nadia paused and thought. 'We can't bury the past forever. We have to take things out, dust them off and really look at them, no matter how uncomfortable it is for us. We make decisions, have beliefs as children, and we store them away, using our child logic. Those beliefs may be true or maybe not, but it was all we could do at that age. And if the thought or memory is painful, we leave it there, in the back of our minds, and never dare touch it for fear of opening old wounds. But the trouble is, it is festering, and now, for you in this case, there is no going back. You've discovered something crucial about yourself, and you can't go on numbing it all as you have done for years, so facing it is the only option. And Sharif and I will help, of course, but ultimately this is your story, and only you can really uncover it. So what are you going to do now?'

'I don't know.' Carmel sighed wearily. 'I wouldn't even know where to start to look for this Joe. I don't even know his surname. And anyway, he may not even be my father. And if he is, he doesn't deserve to have me land up and wreck his life, a reminder of a girl he knew forty years ago. He's probably living happily, and the last thing he'd need is me showing up, destroying everything he's built. He probably doesn't know I exist, or if he knew about Dolly's pregnancy, might not even have told his wife or kids, if he has them.' Carmel fought back the tears and Nadia squeezed her arm.

'I know what you are saying, and I understand, but have you thought about what might happen if he is happy to see you? He might be your father, and you might have a relationship with him, and all I've heard from you is how he doesn't deserve this or that, the damage you could cause to him. What about what you deserve, hmm? Don't you think you deserve something? None of this is your fault. You're the innocent victim in all of this, and I think you deserve a chance to at least find this man. And if you can find him, and I know that's a big if, ask him if he'll take a DNA test. If it proves he's not your father, then so be it – at least he can fill in some more gaps for you about Dolly. And if he is, well then, that's a whole new chapter in your life, Carmel. Everything has been on hold for you for too long. You are entitled to a life. You are entitled to know who your parents are. How can you be a whole person, complete, if you don't know where you've come from?' They stopped walking. 'Ahh, Betty's, my favourite tearoom. Let's rest our legs, shall we?'

Carmel allowed herself to be led into a bright, sunny tearoom and gratefully sank into a booth while Nadia ordered tea and cake.

Maybe there was some truth in what Nadia said, though it felt strange to admit that she had a right to anything. For so much of her life, she was in the way, someone to be taken care of out of duty or necessity. Her needs were met in the most perfunctory of ways – food, clothes, a bed – but nobody ever consulted her on anything or asked her how she felt, what she thought. She was inconsequential. She was always under a compliment to someone, so her own rights never entered into it. But Nadia and Sharif didn't see her that way, and maybe this Joe wouldn't either, if she could find him.

Nadia sat down as the waitress placed cups, a large china teapot and two slices of pear and almond cake from a tray to the table.

'What does Sharif think you should do?' Nadia asked.

'He thinks we should try to find this Joe, and as usual says he'll help me in whatever way he can, but I've taken enough from him already. The last thing he needs is me bringing even more trouble to his door, or causing even more expense and hassle. I should probably just leave well enough alone.'

'Carmel, you have to stop this. I mean it.'

Nadia looked stern and Carmel's stomach lurched. She must have said the wrong thing. She felt her face flush and opened her mouth to apologise when Nadia went on.

'You say Sharif is so far above you and you're causing him trouble or whatever nonsense you just said, but that's just wrong. He loves you, and I have not seen my darling boy in love for so very, very many years. You make him laugh so loudly and so often – it does my heart good to see it. Years ago, he used to be full of fun, and he was such a mischievous child, but in recent years, well, he's had a lot to deal with. He has just been so busy with Aashna and never took time for himself. He just threw himself into his work, and you know what they say about all work and no play?' She chuckled. 'And you love him too, I can see that. Dolly sent him to you. I don't know if you believe in that or not, but I do, and I am sure that Dolly sent Sharif to you. You see it as he rescued you, and yes, he did, but Carmel, you rescued him as well.'

'That's what he says too, but, Nadia, he could have anyone. I mean all the nurses, every woman we meet looks at him and then looks at me and…'

'And they think what a beautiful couple you two make and see how you only have eyes for each other. That's what people see, Carmel, nothing else. But one thing I do know. You have to love yourself before you can truly give or receive love from anyone else. You were never taught to love yourself, and that man you married, well, honestly, I don't know what to say about him as he did nothing to help. But this is the new you, a second chance. Trust Sharif and let him help you.'

Nadia was right. Carmel had read enough self-help books to know that, but the saying of it was one thing; putting it into practice was something else entirely. 'I don't know how to love myself,' she whispered sadly.

'Well, there's the first step.' Nadia topped up the teacups. 'Look around your life now, Carmel. Nobody here apart from Sharif and me know your story and how have they reacted?'

'They're nice, but that's just because of Dolly...' Carmel began, knowing it sounded pathetic, but it was honestly how she felt.

'No, it isn't. They loved Dolly and are glad you're here, definitely, but look at that lad Zane – he thinks you're a scream. He was only telling me the other day about an incident in the gardening class that had the entire place in stitches.'

Carmel remembered. There was an old gardener at Trinity House who was very nice but had a drink problem. He often slept in the potting shed, much to the annoyance of the nuns, but they hadn't the heart to fire him. The nuns brought him into the kitchen for his lunch most days, and as he sipped his tea one afternoon, one of the little girls aged around four eyed him intently. Then she announced to the nun, 'Sister Margaret, I don't know what you mean! Mr Kennedy does not drink like a fish!' Carmel smiled.

'You see? People love you for you. You have such a funny turn of phrase, and you're a natural storyteller. And you are lovely looking...' Seeing the incredulity on Carmel's face, she insisted, 'No, you are. Not an opinion, a fact. But more importantly, you're kind. The patients here love that you attend as many of the activities as you can, you chat to them, you notice who doesn't have many visitors and seek them out and listen to their stories. You find the good in people. You make them feel important. That's a rare gift, Carmel, but as your mother might have said, "'Twasn't from the ground you licked it."'

Carmel laughed to hear the peculiar Irishism from Nadia's lips.

'So try to see yourself as the world does. We all love you, my son adores you, you have great friends here, but you must start to really believe you're worthy of that affection. So will you try?'

Carmel smiled and locked eyes with Nadia. 'I will. I promise.'

CHAPTER 30

*J*ust as they were about to go to bed, Sharif's beeper went off. Immediately, he rang reception. 'Marlena?'

Carmel started clearing up the cups. They'd drunk so much chai tea over a long talk about her past and her future. She explained how she felt, and he understood and empathised. He mirrored his mother's advice, and it felt good to be honest.

'OK, I'm on my way.' He hung up. 'Some people are in reception, quite distressed. Marlena thinks they're Irish – will you come? There's nobody else on tonight, and if people are upset, they might need a soothing voice while I examine the patient.' He was putting on his shoes, the beautiful tan leather slip-on ones she'd admired that first day in Dublin.

'Of course.' She followed him out into the dark night, walking through the grounds and then in through the back entrance of the main building.

Unlike hospitals, Aashna House was kept dark at night. Sharif wanted people to feel as at home as possible. They walked in silence along the corridor.

In reception, two men waited, both in their seventies, she guessed. One was sitting on a chair, seemingly in great pain, and the other rested his hand on his companion's shoulder, clearly worried sick by the look on his face. When he saw Sharif and Carmel, he immediately came forward. 'I'm sorry for the late call, and I know you don't have an A & E here, but my friend is in terrible pain… He has cancer…'

'No problem. Carmel, can you get a wheelchair please?' Sharif bent down in front of the man in the chair. 'I'm Dr Sharif Khan. I'd like to examine you if I may, so I'm going to take you to an examination room and we can take it from there.'

The man looked up and nodded, the pain etching deep lines on his face. 'I know who you are. Dolly told me to come here when it got too bad,' he croaked.

Carmel froze. Sharif caught her eye but said nothing; his focus was on the man in front of him. Dolly? There could only be one Dolly. Did this man know her mother too?

Sharif's voice cut through her shock. 'Carmel, if you can just help me to get Mr…?'

'Brian, Brian McDaid.'

Every word was agony for the poor man, so Carmel's questions would have to wait. Together, they lifted him into the wheelchair, and Sharif pushed him into an examination room down the corridor. Carmel followed, and once there, they had to help him onto the bed. Carmel withdrew then to allow Sharif to examine him, stepping back into the corridor where the other man watched in wordless despair. He was tall and distinguished, in a long navy wool coat and a trilby hat, which he rotated nervously in his hands.

'Would you like a cup of tea? Dr Khan could be a while, and he'll page me when he's ready. I'm Carmel. I work here.' Carmel offered her hand and the man shook it.

'Tim O'Flaherty. Yes, a cup of tea would be nice. I suppose I can't just stand here…'

The poor man looked distraught with worry, and Carmel wondered what the connection was between him and Brian McDaid. She led him to the small coffee dock in the main building and put on the kettle. Tim sat, but she could tell he was beside himself.

'So is Brian family?' she asked gently.

'Er, yes, sort of. We…ah, we live together.'

Carmel took that to mean they were in a relationship. Something about the man's appearance, the elegant way he dressed, the clear distress he was in at Brian's condition convinced her.

'Is that a trace of an Irish accent I hear?' she asked, trying to keep his mind off his partner.

'Yes.' He half smiled. 'From County Mayo originally, but I've been here over fifty years. And you?'

'Dublin, and Offaly after that.' She knew she shouldn't pry, but she couldn't help herself. 'So what made you come here rather than A & E?'

'A friend of ours, well, of Brian's, really, used to have a connection here. She was a friend of Dr Khan's family, and when she got sick, she was a patient. I've been looking after him at home for the last five years, but Dolly – that was our friend – said that when it got too much, we should come here. Brian hates hospitals, so I've promised to try to keep him out of them. Tonight, well, he was in such pain, and the meds just weren't touching it. I hated taking him out of our house, but I was scared…'

'You did the right thing. We don't have an emergency department as such, but Dr Khan is an oncologist and he'll be able to make him comfortable. Try not to worry.' Despite Carmel's longing to know if the Dolly he spoke about was her mother, she knew that it wasn't fair to cross-examine the man at this point.

'Will he be able to come back home, do you think?' Tim asked, then immediately he apologised. 'I'm sorry, how would you know? I just… He'd rather be at home.'

Carmel handed him a cup of tea and a Kit Kat. 'This place, Aashna, it's not really like a hospital. It doesn't smell like one or even really look like one. I've no idea about whether he can go home or not – that will be up to him and Dr Kahn will advise him – but if Brian does end up coming here, it will be OK, I promise you.'

'It's the beginning of the end. I've known for a few months now. Dolly used to visit us a few times a week, and she'd give me a break, let me get out to the bank or shopping or whatever, and she'd stay with him. She and Brian knew each other since they were children – they grew up in Dublin together. He took her death really badly. He's been going downhill since she died, to be honest.'

Carmel's heart thumped wildly in her chest. It had to be her Dolly. It just had to be. Just as she was about to ask him something else, Sharif beeped her. 'We can go back now. He's ready to see you.'

Tim rose immediately and followed Carmel down the dimly lit corridor. The little room she showed him into was cosy, and Brian was in the bed, eyes closed and sleeping peacefully, looking considerably less distressed than twenty minutes earlier.

'I've administered some analgesic, a strong morphine-based painkiller, so he'll be comfortable enough for the night. I suggest that you leave him here for now. We'll take good care of him, and perhaps you could come back tomorrow. I'll do some tests, and we can take it from there?' Sharif's voice had a soothing effect on patients and families alike.

Tim seemed relieved to see Brian so peaceful. He crossed to the bed, and Sharif and Carmel left the room to allow him a few minutes alone.

Carmel waited as Sharif entered the details on the computer at reception, giving instructions to Marlene as to what care Brian would need for the night. The examination room was, like all of the rooms at Aashna, fitted out with a proper bed, not a gurney, and it would be quite comfortable for the night for Brian. He arranged a series of tests for the following morning and asked the night nursing staff to add Brian to their rounds.

Tim appeared a few moments later. 'Thank you, Dr Khan. Yes, I'll go home now, and I'll see you tomorrow. Thank you for taking care of him. He was in terrible pain...'

'He'll be fine now. From a preliminary exam and from what Brian was able to tell me, I can see he is in the later stages of his cancer, so I must prepare you – I think all we can do at this stage is palliative. But as I said, we'll talk about it properly tomorrow. If you can bring a list of medications he's currently taking and the details of your GP, I'll liaise with them and we'll make sure he is given the best possible care.'

'Will he be able to come home, do you think?' Tim asked, and Carmel's heart went out to him.

'Well, that ultimately will be up to him and to you,' Sharif explained kindly, 'but let's have a chat tomorrow and we can take it from there. Try to get some sleep. It's been a hard time for you, I can see. Can we call a taxi for you?'

'No. I'm fine. I drove. Thank you, though.' Tim smiled sadly and shook Sharif's hand. 'Thank you both again.'

Once Tim had gone, Sharif and Carmel started the walk back to their apartment.

'I think he knew my mother,' Carmel blurted once they were outside. 'Tim, Brian's partner, told me that Brian and Dolly grew up together in Dublin and they were friends and that she died here recently.'

'I know. He did know her. She used to visit them regularly. Brian managed to tell me that, despite his pain. We always wondered where she went, and now that I know, it seems even stranger. Why didn't she tell us about them? She would have known that the fact that they are gay wouldn't have bothered me or my parents, so it can't be that.' Sharif was as puzzled as she was. He stopped and turned to her. 'Carmel, I know you want to know everything and that this is hard for you, but Dolly had her reasons for not telling us about her relationship with them, and maybe they feel the same. I want to ask him everything too, believe me. But he is a very sick man, so if he wants to talk, it has to be in his own time, OK?'

She nodded. Sharif knew how much finding out about her parents meant to her, but he was this man's doctor first and foremost.

'OK. I know. I won't go in there first thing in the morning with a list of questions, I promise.'

He smiled and kissed the top of her head.

CHAPTER 31

*C*armel slept fitfully in the days after Brian's admission, so many questions going round her head. Tim came the next day, and he and Brian and Sharif had a meeting. Of course, she wasn't privy to what went on; Sharif never discussed his patients with anyone.

He knew she was worried and said Brian had not mentioned anything about Dolly since being admitted but that he didn't feel it fair to ask, so they had only discussed his medical situation. Sharif promised that if he mentioned anything about Dolly, he'd ask if he could relay it to her, but said that he couldn't bring it up. A week after Brian was admitted, she decided to ask Sharif if she could see him herself. He was in the high-dependency wing and was still very sick, but she was going out of her mind. What if he died? Maybe anything he could tell her about her mother, maybe even her father, would die with him. She felt awful for being so selfish, but she was so scared her one chance was slipping away.

She went about her business as normal, but she longed to speak to him. Tim came and went, but he was so upset and worried, it wasn't right to bother him with her questions, and anyway she wanted to speak to Brian directly; he was the connection with Dolly, not his partner. Sharif knew how she felt, but Brian was just too weak.

'I don't know,' he said. 'I want to help you, Carmel, of course I do, and I'm dying to know myself too, but it feels wrong to me, unethical, you know? Look, I'll ask him if he'll see you. To be honest, he's rarely awake – the medication needed to control the pain means he is sedated most of the time – but mid-morning is the time he is at his most alert. I know how much this means to you. And in any other circumstances, I'd absolutely refuse to have anyone visit him that wasn't immediate family, but I'll see what I can do. I'm not promising anything, though, all right? It has to be up to him. He's very ill but not in imminent danger of death, so maybe if I can get his symptoms under control a bit better, he would be in better shape.'

'I understand. And thanks, Sharif.'

She and Sharif had bought two chairs and a table for their little courtyard, and she'd planted some flowers in pots. They loved to have coffee there on the mornings when they were off work, and read the papers or just chat quietly. He'd moved his things into their apartment, letting his own go to a family who needed to be with their fifteen-year-old daughter who was dying of leukaemia. Her name was Debbie, and it seemed so wrong that her life would be cut short so cruelly. Sharif's presence seemed to soothe people, though, and Carmel marvelled at how he could make Debbie laugh.

Carmel was also amazed at his wardrobe. He had so many things that the entire wardrobe in the guest room was his alone.

The night he arrived with a box of personal things, she tried not to flinch when he removed a gilt-framed photo of a beautiful young Asian woman and placed it on the table along with some books and clothes.

He caught her looking at it. 'That's Jamilla. I told you about her.'

She could hear the sadness in his voice and once more was transported back to the kitchen in Ballyshanley, dusting carefully around the picture of Bill and Gretta. She knew it wasn't the same, but she couldn't help the feeling of resentment. Was she to start again, with another dead woman gazing at her every day?

'I can put it away if it makes you feel uncomfortable.'

Instantly, Carmel felt mean and cruel. Why should he be forced to forget his past? 'Of course not. Don't be silly.' She picked up the photo and looked deeply into Jamilla's brown eyes. 'She was beautiful.'

'She was. And funny and kind, just like you actually. You would have liked her. When she died, I thought I'd never recover. The pain, every day…and the fact that I was a doctor but couldn't save her – it ate away at me. Maybe that's why I threw myself so completely into this place. That's what my mother thinks, I know, that I was using work to numb the loss. Maybe she was right. I would work so hard that when I fell into bed at night, I had no energy for thinking, for feeling, and so that was my life for so long. But time eases everything, even if you don't want it to, and one day it hurt a little less and so on, until I was in a position to live again. And then I met you.'

'Let's put her here, on the shelf. That way you can see her every day.' Carmel tried to inject enthusiasm into her voice.

'I have a better idea,' he said, gently taking the photo from her. 'How about we put it on the shelf in the spare bedroom? I don't need to see her every day, but sometimes it's nice to see her smile. I'd hate to put it in a drawer or something, but we cannot live in the past – we must live in the here and now.'

'Are you sure?' It was like he could read her mind.

'Totally sure. I loved Jamilla once, so very much. But she's gone and we are here, and she wouldn't want me to dwell on her. A little part of me will always be hers – I told you that before – but most of me, the part that's alive and loving life, is all yours. Jamilla is no threat to you, Carmel, I promise you.'

Sharif had smiled when he saw her a few mornings later in her dressing gown. He'd come home for tea after his early rounds. She was curled up with a cup of tea in the courtyard reading a book. The morning sun was trapped in the little space.

'You look so happy here.' He kissed the top of her head and joined her.

'I'm sorry, I should get dressed.' She was embarrassed and began to gather her things to go inside.

'Why? I thought you were not in until eleven today? It's only nine thirty.'

She relaxed; he was right. This was her apartment, and there were no bells or nuns or anyone else telling her what to do or when to do it. But old habits died hard. 'All right, I'll slob around for another while then.' She grinned. 'It feels so wrong, but I'm determined to be more slovenly. When I was a kid, all the time I was in Trinity House actually, you got up on the first bell at 7 a.m., got washed and dressed before the second bell at 7:20, had your bed made and were sitting at the table for breakfast by the third bell at 7:40. When I married Bill, it was the same, more or less. He had his breakfast after milking, but he had tea and a bowl of porridge at 5:30, so I'm used to being up and ready. This lounging around business is new to me.' She grinned to dispel the sadness that had crept across his handsome face. She reminded herself not to tell him any more stories of her childhood; it only made him sad.

'Even on the weekends? Were you not allowed to lie in, or play?'

Carmel put her hand on his. 'It wasn't "Oliver Twist", you know. We didn't have to work on a big wheel or up chimneys. It was fine. We did play sometimes. After dinner when the clear-up was done, the nuns would let us play cards or there were some board games we could use, and the boys went outside to kick a football. They taught me to sew and to knit. It honestly wasn't that bad.'

'Please tell me Bill didn't expect you to get up and feed him every day?' Sharif rarely said anything about Bill, and never criticised him, so Carmel was a little taken aback.

'Well, he kind of told me the schedule the first day, and I just did it and…well, kept doing it, I suppose. He didn't demand it or anything – it was just how things were done. I never saw him make so much a a cup of tea in all the years, I don't know if he would know how. Though how he's surviving now is anyone's guess, I suppose the wicked witch of the west has moved in and is boiling up eye of toad and spleen of newt soup every night before taking off on her broomstick.'

Sharif chuckled and she went on,

'Anyway, when he went milking, then I'd do the housework, and sometimes listen to a podcast or a meditation. I could only do that when I was sure he wouldn't be back, though. He'd have had a stroke if he found me meditating, probably taken me down to Father Linehan to have me exorcised or something.' She giggled but this time Sharif didn't smile.

He locked eyes with her as if looking behind them into her mind, her soul. Once, she told him he reminded her of Deepak Chopra, an Indian-born alternative medicine practitioner. Not in the way he looked as such, apart from them coming from similar countries, but there was something deeply spiritual about Sharif. He could be still for long periods and was very connected to himself. He had studied philosophy for many years and continued to do so, and he was a deep thinker while also being full of fun and mischief. It was one of the many reasons she loved him so much.

'Will you divorce him?'

The question caught her off guard. 'Em...I don't know. We were married in the Catholic Church, but divorce is legal now...' She had never really considered it. If she thought about it at all, then maybe she thought he would get his marriage to her annulled.

'Carmel, I'm not trying to pressure you. If you're not ready, then that's fine. But you could easily see a solicitor here and start divorce proceedings. You don't need a reason, though the fact that the marriage was never consummated would probably be grounds for a legal annulment.'

'But what would he say? He'd be horrified to get a letter from England, from a solicitor. I mean, I did the wrong thing here. I left him without so much as a note. I don't think I should be the one to –'

'You did not do anything wrong!' Sharif was unusually impatient. 'Listen to yourself, Carmel! You blame yourself for everything. You got dealt a terrible hand in life. It was wrong, and you deserved better. You weren't adopted, and that was wrong. Bill married you when he wasn't emotionally available. That was wrong. He treated you like a servant. That was wrong. He didn't nurture a relationship between his daughters and you. That was wrong. He allowed his witchy sister to bully you and undermine you, and that was wrong. You are not the perpetrator in any of this – you're the victim, and you have got a chance now to leave all those wrongs in the past. You are entitled to free yourself from him, legally and mentally, and you should do it. Who cares what he thinks, or what people in the village think? He is the one with something to hide. He's the one who should be hanging his head in shame.' Sharif, normally so soothing, logical and calm was unusually worked up.

Carmel stood and went to sit on his lap, and he put his arms around her. Smoothing his silver hair from his temples, she spoke directly to him. 'I'm convinced my mother sent you to me, though I wish she'd sent you a few years earlier, as it would have been even better. But maybe I wasn't in the place where I could accept you into my life then – who knows? It must seem ridiculous, a grown woman so unsure of herself. I understand the logic of everything you say, I really do. If someone else told me the story of my life, I'd be like, "Oh, for goodness' sake, she needs a kick in the arse", as we say in Ireland, but it's not that simple. For so long, all my life really, I wasn't important to anyone. That sounds a bit whiney maybe, but it's true. I'm not feeling sorry for myself – I just wasn't loved. And because nobody loved me, or at least nobody I was aware of – I know now that my mother never stopped loving me and that makes such a difference – I'm not used to it. I didn't expect anything from Bill. I mean, sure, at the start I foolishly thought we could live happily ever after, but the reality was that was never going to happen. He shouldn't have married me, but he saved me. I know it must sound awful to you, the life I had with him, and it was awful in so many ways – it was. But then I'd see documentaries about homeless people or drug addicts, and so often they grew up in state care, and when they reached adulthood, they were just thrown out into the world with no skills. And I'd think, well, at least Bill saved me from that. I had a roof over my head and enough to eat, and people thought of me as a normal person, with a home and a family. And when you don't have that, ever, then it's something precious.'

She really wanted him to understand so went on. 'You can't really get it. You had parents who adored you and a huge extended family, so you knew where you belonged from the start. It's different when you spend your life trying to find a place to be, when everyone else has their spot and you don't. I remember at school one time we were learning about the cuckoo, and how he never had a nest of his own but used to steal other birds' nests. The teacher was making out like he was a bad bird compared to all the others who worked so hard on their nests, then the cuckoo came along and just jumped into it. But I remember thinking, what else was he to do? If you don't have a nest of your own, then you have to try to muscle in on someone else's. The cuckoo never learned nest building because his parents never built nests either, so it wasn't really his fault. All my life, I've been a cuckoo, and that's why I try not to make too many waves or upset people – it's because I'm always the encroacher. So I know I'm hard to understand. And I will divorce Bill – I'd love to have him out of my life. Don't think for a second that I feel in any way connected to him, because I'm not. But when you say you love me, or even when I look around our lovely home, sometimes I don't believe it. I'm afraid that you are going to stop loving me when the novelty wears off or some-thing…though I'm hardly a novelty, but you know what I mean. I'm sorry. It must be such a head wreck, as Zane calls it, to be dealing with me.'

Sharif sighed and patted her shoulder, indicating he wanted her to get up. Again, the panic – had she said something wrong? Should she have kept her mouth shut? Maybe he was getting sick of her stupid insecurities. He went into their bedroom and emerged moments later. She was rooted to the spot as he came out through the French doors back into the little courtyard.

Carmel stood in amazement in her dressing gown and slippers as the man she loved got down on one knee in front of her.

'Carmel, I don't want you to be a cuckoo any more. I want us to have a nest together. I hate the idea that you're afraid that I'll change my mind or go off you or something. I love you so much, and I want to be your home and for you to be mine. I know you're not free yet, but when you are, will you marry me?'

He held up a little box containing an exquisite ring, a gold spiral encrusted with diamonds and rubies. It was breathtaking.

'Sharif, I...I don't know what to say...' She could hardly get the words out. She looked down at this gorgeous man, and her heart felt too big for her chest. 'I would absolutely love to marry you.'

CHAPTER 32

The following day Sharif beeped her. Brian was well enough for a short visit. She rushed across the campus from the Kaivalya, where she had welcomed the local Toastmasters group for their monthly debate, and headed to the high-dependency wing.

Sharif met her in the corridor. 'Don't tire him out now – keep it short. Maybe you can see him again tomorrow or the next day. Talking will exhaust him.' He bent his head and kissed her quickly. 'Good luck.'

Carmel nodded; she was too nervous to speak. Gathering all her resolve, she knocked gently on the door.

'Come in.' The voice was strong, and the accent unmistakably Dublin.

She was relieved to see how well Brian looked, sitting up in a chair, in his own clothes. He was bald from the chemotherapy; he had no eyebrows or eyelashes either. But his complexion had much more colour than it had the night he was admitted.

'Hello, Mr McDaid, and thank you so much for seeing me. I know it's tiring to have visitors, so I won't keep you long, and if you get too tired, please just tell me to go.' Carmel tried to keep the nervousness from her voice.

'Not at all. I've been waiting to meet you. When Dr Khan told me who you were, well, I couldn't believe my ears. He told me you were never adopted and that you didn't know why. Well, I think I might be able to explain.' He smiled, and Carmel warmed to him instantly.

'Sit down there on the bed so I can see you. You're the head cut off your mother – that's the truth. I'll tell you what I know, Carmel. I would have come sooner if I'd known you were here, but I must warn you, it's not a happy story.' He waited for her to respond.

'Please, whatever it is, I want to know.'

'OK. Well, your ma and me were great mates and we got along so well. I knew her since we were kids, even though there was a long gap in the middle when we didn't see each other for years. Anyway, I'll get to that. Are you sure you want to hear this? Once you hear it, you can't ever not know it, y'know?' His Dublin accent was strong and reminded her of the delivery men who used to come to Trinity House.

She nodded. 'Please, go on.'

Brian inhaled almost as if to gather his strength. Sharif was managing his pain, but she could see he was bone-weary of it all. He began, staring straight ahead of him as he spoke. 'Dolly, your ma, was going out with my brother Joe since she was sixteen, childhood sweethearts as they used to say long ago. We all grew up together, on the same road in Kilmainham – Dolly, me, Joe, Kevin and Colm, my sisters Maggie and Orla, and a few other families. When Dolly's mother died – she was only a kid – and Austin, her father, went to pieces, it was to our house she came. My ma would feed her, wash her clothes, all of that. My father never liked her, even as a child, said she was flighty, but we took no notice of him. He could only talk with his fists or his belt, and we all, including my mother, got the wrong end of it often. He was a bad man, evil. He wasn't a drinker. If he was, you could blame that, but he just was a cruel man. He gave us all a hard time, but poor old Joe got the worst of it. I didn't know why at the time, but later Joe told me he walked in on him attacking our mother. Joe was only twelve, but he was a big strong lad and he hit him a clatter so hard he put the auld fella in hospital for a month.' Brian paused and took a sip of water.

'He broke his jaw, and me da hit his head off the range as he fell. Joe could have killed him, so ferocious the blow was. Guards, social workers, the whole lot got involved then and it all came out. You know what Ireland's like, and on a street like ours, where everyone was stuck in everyone else's business anyway, well, the place was buzzing. To be honest, I think some of the neighbours suspected. We, and Ma, would regularly appear with bruises and sometimes broken bones, but nobody said anything. It was weird. They'd talk about the neighbours all day long, but then when he was clearly battering all of us, people did nothing. Domestic violence was seen as something to be kept within the four walls. I don't know. It's a kind of screwed-up way of thinking over there sometimes. But my father never turned a hair. He'd walk into Mass, Ma with him, and her with a black eye or her arm in a sling, but he'd look like butter wouldn't melt. He was the pillar of the community, you see, collecting the money at Mass, singing in the choir and all that. After that, though, people knew him for what he really was – a bully and a coward. People didn't look up to him any more. He never forgave Joe for that.' He stopped, composing himself, as if gathering inner strength.

'We can stop if you like...' Carmel said, though she longed to hear whatever it was he had to say.

He snorted a laugh. 'I doubt I've much time left, so I better get on with it.'

'If you're sure?' Carmel felt awful putting him under pressure like this.

'I'm grand. Anyway, Dolly and Joe had a special bond or something. When she smiled, his face lit up like Cleary's window at Christmas. Since they were kids, you'd never see one without the other. It was almost as if they had a secret language or something. It's hard to explain, but for Joe, there was never another, and I think the same was true for Dolly. Anyway, once she got to sixteen, she was allowed to go out with Joe. Austin, Dolly's da, wasn't happy about it – he was very strict even by the standards of those times – but Dolly convinced him, and anyway, he liked Joe. Austin had no time for my father either and probably was secretly proud of how Joe handled him.' Brian stopped and took another sip of water, composing himself once more.

'Joe was apprenticed to a butcher on Capel Street and Dolly was working in the Arnotts drapery department – that's where she learned to sew. They were stone mad about each other. He walked her to work and collected her every day. They'd walk all over Dublin in the evenings, just talking. Other girls liked Joe too – he was a good-looking lad – but he was oblivious. They were going out for years and they never bored of each other – he would rather be with her than anyone. They had great plans to travel the world once they'd saved up enough money.

'I remember there was a ferocious fuss made one night when Austin came home early from whatever thing he was at and found Joe and Dolly in bed. He nearly went mental and banned Joe from the house. That sort of thing was unthinkable in those days, even though by now they were in their twenties.

'Joe begged and pleaded with him, trying to convince him that he wasn't just using his daughter, that he loved her. Dolly loved her da and was sorry she disappointed him. Eventually Austin thawed, and after a few weeks, they were back together again. The auld fella probably knew that Dolly'd defy him if she had to anyway. Nothing would keep her and my brother apart.

'We were sure that the ring would be produced for Christmas that year. In fact, I knew Joe had planned to propose because the girl our brother Colm was doing a line with was roped in to check the sizes of the rings in McDowell's on O'Connell Street.

'Christmas Eve came, and both Dolly and Joe were working late. Ma was in the kitchen getting everything ready for Christmas dinner, and the girls were up to ninety about Santa coming and all of that. Us older ones chipped in to get their stuff because my father would have nothing to do with it. Joe was going to bring Dolly home with him after work and was going to propose on the way.

'Instead of the big announcement, though, Joe appeared at the back door, ashen-faced. He said that Dolly was gone. He'd waited for her at work, and they said she'd not turned up. He went to her house, and her father was sitting at the table with a note from her saying she was gone. No note for Joe, no explanation, just a two-line thing to her father saying she was sorry but that she was leaving.

'Joe nearly went out of his mind. He just couldn't believe that she'd just up and leave him without a word. We shared a room, and at night I used to hear him crying over her. She broke his heart, so she did. He couldn't understand it – none of us could. Poor old Austin Mullane lost the will to go on after that. Losing his wife and then Dolly was too much for him to bear. He used to walk all over Dublin looking for her. He wrote to the police in England and even contacted some agency in America to see if she could be found, but it was as if she'd vanished into thin air.

'She never contacted Joe or her father ever again, never even a letter, nothing. Austin died about four years after she left, a heart attack. Then one day, about six years ago, I saw her here, on Tottenham Court Road, in a draper's shop. I couldn't believe my eyes, but it was definitely Dolly. It had been decades, but I knew it was her.

'I went in and confronted her, and she nearly collapsed. I was so angry at what she'd done to poor Joe, I let her have it. I told her about all the misery she'd caused him, and about her poor father and what she put him through. She closed the shop and told me to sit down. That was when she told me about you.' Brian leaned back against the pillow. The effort of so much talking was weakening him, Carmel could see.

'We really can leave it if you want to...' she offered. She remembered her promise to Sharif.

He sipped some more water and took a deep breath. 'No, I want to tell you this. You've a right to know.'

'All right, thank you.' Carmel swallowed, hardly able to bear the suspense.

'OK, so even then I was mad. I shouted at her that she could have told Joe and they'd have brought the wedding forward – they wouldn't have been the first couple to do that – but then she broke down. Just started crying. And, well, I was never one for crying women, so I just sat there. Eventually she told me that the reason she left without a word was that the child – you – might not have been Joe's.'

Blood thundered in Carmel's ears. What was he saying? She struggled to focus, telling herself she would have time to think about it all afterwards; for now she had to hear the story.

'I couldn't believe what she was telling me. They were always together and she never had eyes for anyone else, so I was totally confused until she told me who your father was, or could be anyway. Are you sure you want me to go on with this? As I said, there are some things people are better off not knowing.'

Carmel just nodded. She couldn't speak with the lump in her throat. She blinked back the tears; she didn't want to say or do anything that would make him stop.

He took a moment to compose his thoughts; whatever he was going to tell her wasn't coming easily to him. He sipped his water again. The silence hung heavily between them. When he spoke his voice sounded different; there was a hard edge that hadn't been there before. 'Apparently my father got wind that Joe was going to propose to Dolly, must have overheard something about the ring, and decided he'd hurt Joe in the most terrible way. Get his revenge on him for what my father saw as Joe's ruining of his life. My father never took responsibility for anything he did, not to his dying day. As he saw it, Joe had destroyed his reputation, and so he would hurt him by taking the thing he loved the most. He waited for Dolly on her way home from work a few weeks before Christmas. Joe said he was working late that night so Dolly was to go home without him. It was dark, and my father waited and dragged her into the trees of Saint Canice's Park. Well, you can guess what came next.'

Carmel felt sick. A wave of cold washed over her, and she was sure she was going to vomit. She didn't, and the nausea subsided, but cold sweat prickled her back. The idea of continuing the conversation terrified and revolted her, but she knew she had to hear it all. Taking a few gulps of air to steady herself, she managed to croak, 'Go on.'

'I'm not telling you this to be cruel, but you wanted to know... The weeks went on and Dolly knew she was pregnant. She wasn't sure which one of them was your father. In a panic, she told my father. To the day she died, she regretted that. If only she'd told Joe or even her own father, but telling our da was the worst mistake she could have made. He knew Dolly would never tell Joe that she'd been raped, especially by his own father – she'd be scared what Joe would do. He reminded Dolly that since Joe had attacked him before and the Guards were involved, if Joe assaulted him again, Joe could face charges. And Dolly knew Joe could do worse than assault him – she was afraid Joe would kill him for what he'd done.'

Was this really her story? Rape. She was a child of rape. Her poor mother. No wonder she left. A million thoughts scrambled for supremacy in Carmel's mind, but she dragged her focus back to the man in the bed. 'That's horrendous,' was all she could manage.

'It was, and he used her love of my brother, her fear that he would pay the price for murder if he found out the truth. My old man saw how panicked Dolly was. Ireland was a harsh place for girls who got themselves 'in trouble', as they said, even if through no fault of their own. He threatened her that if she said anything to Joe, then Joe would kill him and go to prison for the murder. He then went on to terrify her about what a public trial like that would do to Austin. She told me that day that she just couldn't do it, be responsible for Joe going to jail, for destroying her father. She said that my father was apparently pleased she was pregnant, delighted he'd caused maximum pain to Joe, and it was he who delivered Dolly to the nuns where you were born.'

Though his words told a horrible story, his eyes were kind. Carmel knew he didn't want to hurt her, but he had to tell her the truth and she had to hear it. She could see him tiring, but he was determined to go on.

'She didn't see our father again until two days before he died, five years ago. He lived to be ninety-seven. She'd read a piece about him written in the local paper online. Apparently, for years she used to subscribe to the actual paper and had it delivered to her in England, and then it went online so she'd read it every week. It's mostly pictures of kids and football teams, but she said it felt like a small connection with her home. Anyway, because my father was still very involved with the Church for years after the incident, someone wrote a tribute piece about him, pillar of the community and all the usual rubbish. Anyway, Dolly read it, and whoever wrote it said that the parish sends their best wishes to him in the Mater Hospital and all of that, so she knew where he was.

'So your mam went to see him, in secret, of course. She was beginning to think that somehow he had something to do with her inability to find you, though what, she couldn't imagine. She described going over to Dublin and going into the hospital. She waited until late at night when she was sure none of the other family would be there, and she went into the room to him. She saw him lying there, ravaged by time and sickness, and demanded to know what had happened to you. He laughed at her misery – can you imagine that? She told him about all the years spent looking for you, and he cackled, and then he told her the truth. That after he dropped her at the unmarried mother's home, he went in to have tea with the Reverend Mother. Of course he said nothing to the nun about raping his son's girlfriend, but just that he'd been indiscreet, that she'd flirted with him and he foolishly succumbed to her wanton ways. The nun readily believed him and almost had sympathy for him when he explained that he was a married man who didn't want his wife and children upset by this little mistake. He asked them to take care of things short term, and that he'd be grateful. He paid them, you see. Nuns would turn a blind eye to almost anything for money in those days. He told the nun that he might, in time, convince his wife to take pity on the child and allow it to live with them, so in the meantime, no permission for adoption was to be given under any circumstances. He said nobody was to be told of your existence – he ensured it was written on your file. I suppose that when you were sent on to wherever they sent babies that weren't adopted, it would have remained on it, so that's probably why you were never adopted and Dolly wasn't allowed access to you. It was an awful, cruel, mean system, but I think that's what happened.' Brian stopped and reached out for Carmel's hand. 'Is this too hard? I can stop...'

'No, please go on.' Her words were barely audible. 'My birth certificate. I asked for one when I was applying for my passport, and the one they gave me had "unknown" written under the word "father". My birth mother's name was written as Mary Murphy. How could they have done that?'

'I've no idea, but as we now know, babies born in those places were adopted all over the world without proper paperwork, so they were a bit of a law unto themselves, I think.'

Carmel tried to absorb all this information. Brian was exhausted; she knew she should let him rest. She was about to say as much when he went on.

'Well, that's all there is to know really. Except that I tried to convince her to make contact with Joe, that he'd love to hear from her, even after all these years, but no way. She refused. Nothing I could say would change her mind. Joe was married and happy and had a couple of kids, and she said she didn't want to drop a bomb like that into his happy life. I said I thought he'd see it differently, but she made me swear to never tell him.'

'And Joe, he's still alive?' Carmel wiped her eye with the back of her hand.

'Oh, yes, in Dublin. His wife died of pancreatic cancer about four years ago. Mary. She was a lovely lady. He has a son and a daughter, Jennifer and Luke. They'd be in their thirties now, I'd say. I promised Dolly I'd never tell Joe, but I never said anything about you because she believed you were lost to her forever.'

He rested his head back again, and Carmel could see the toll talking so long was taking.

'Thanks, Brian, for telling me. I...I don't really know what I'm going to do, if anything, but things are making a bit more sense now. Thank you.' She squeezed his hand, and he nodded in return.

'She'd have been so happy to meet you. She talked about you all the time,' he said, his voice weaker now.

'So everyone says. I wish I'd met her too.'

CHAPTER 33

*C*armel woke late the next morning, her throat sore and her eyes swollen from crying. She was overwhelmed from the emotion of it all. Sharif was at the clinic, but he'd left a bunch of freesias, her favourite flowers, by the bed. Beside them was a note saying, *I'm sorry I wasn't here to talk to you about Brian – text me when you wake. I love you. xxx*

He'd been run off his feet the previous days and had crawled into bed in the small hours. She felt him but didn't say anything – she hadn't been ready to talk – and he was gone when she woke. She wanted time to tell him her story, not a quick ten minutes between patients or after he'd worked a sixteen-hour day.

She lay there, thinking once again how lucky she was to have him. Just as she was psyching herself up to get in the shower, her phone buzzed. It was Marlena on reception. *Mr McDaid wants to see you, Carmel. He's very insistent, says he must see you ASAP.*

Immediately, she jumped from the bed. *I'm on the way,* she typed.

She dressed quickly. She looked a fright, she knew, but she didn't care. Running through the grounds, she wondered what more Brian could have to tell her. She tapped in, using her card, to the high-dependency unit and knocked gently on Brian's door.

'Come in.' His voice sounded even weaker than yesterday.

She felt a pang of guilt. She shouldn't have allowed him to exert himself so much. 'Hi, Brian...' She spoke quietly and sat beside the bed.

'How are you? I've been thinking about you and wondering how you were. I've been thinking I shouldn't have said anything. I was wrong to...' A fit of coughing overtook him, and Carmel could see a physical deterioration in him even since yesterday.

'Please don't think that,' she assured him. 'I'm glad you did. Thank you. It wasn't easy, but at least now I know.'

'But you don't know, you see, and neither did your mother, the pain it all caused Joe. I love all my brothers and sisters, but Joe and I were very close – we still are – and there are things I've kept from him, not just this. It wasn't that I couldn't tell him...but...' The effort was racking his body, but he was determined to go on. 'I thought I could convince her to talk to Joe at least, but when she said no...it just...' He was out of breath.

'I know. It's been going round and round in my head all night that Joe might be my father. There's a chance that he is, and he's still alive... I feel like I want to tell him, have a test. Maybe he is my father, but he doesn't even know I exist.'

Brian gestured that she open the drawer beside his bed, afraid to talk in case it precipitated another bout of coughing. She opened it, and lying there among a few other personal effects was a small note-book. He nodded and she handed it to him. She watched as his hands, bruised from all the needles, bony fingers covered in almost translucent skin, flicked through the pages until he came to an address. He handed it to her.

Joe McDaid

14 Firgrove Lawn, Kiltipper Road, Dublin 24 +35384923567

She looked at him. 'But I can't just show up, or ring him or whatever. He mightn't want to hear from me at all. He doesn't even know I exist, let alone that he might have some connection to me.'

'Your choice.' His breathing was laboured. 'That's where to find him if you want to. He'll be here anyway soon enough when I die, so you can see him then.' He lay back on the pillows, his complexion ashen and waxy; he looked so much worse than yesterday. She wondered why his family weren't there already, but apparently he didn't want any visitors but Tim.

He was going downhill fast, but Sharif said that often happened. As a specialist in palliative care, he'd explained that he saw enough to be sure that once someone decided they had had enough of living, they could shut themselves down. Medicine from that point on could only keep someone alive artificially. Once the spirit rests, then so too does the body. She had learned so much about life and death from Sharif, and he had very definite ideas about dignity and honesty around death and dying.

Brian knew exactly the situation regarding his cancer and how aggressive it was. Sharif thought it condescending to lie or soften the truth of a person's illness. It was their life, their body, not their child's or spouse's or whoever, and they had the right to decide for themselves. It often led to disagreements between him and families, but he was a committed advocate for his patient, nobody else.

He also believed that people often needed to face their own death before they felt the need to resolve issues, and sometimes people who were never fully aware of how imminent their death was died at loggerheads with family, or having not put something right. But those who managed to right the wrongs or say what they needed to say seemed to then give themselves the leave to fade away. Sharif said it was almost tangible, that moment when the body says to the spirit, 'You're free to go.'

Brian's eyes were closed now, and Carmel wondered if she should stay or go. Then she realised something. This man was either her uncle or her brother. The reality of it hit her. She sat beside him and held his hand, gently giving him a squeeze, just so he'd know she was there. She might have imagined it, but she thought he squeezed hers back. Eventually, his laboured breathing became rhythmic and slow. When she was sure he was sleeping, she stood. The address book still lay on the bed. Before she had time to change her mind, she pulled out her phone and took a picture of the page. Then she slipped out.

She rushed home, showered and went to work. There were Italian classes and a cookery demonstration going on that day. She met Sharif in the corridor; he was rushing. He stopped and apologised again.

'It's OK, honestly. You're flat out, I know you are. I'll see you at home when you finish, OK?' She squeezed his hand.

'I've a locum in for me tonight, so I'll be back by seven, I promise. Are you OK?'

She smiled at him. 'I'm fine. See you later.'

The day passed quickly, and she popped in several times to check on Brian, who was sleeping peacefully. Tim was there too and they had a quick word; she didn't know how much of what Brian had told her had been shared with Tim, so they kept the conversation light. That evening, she sipped a cup of tea in their courtyard and thought about her mother, allowing her full story to sink in. The lavender and lilacs growing in pots scented the summer's evening. The day had been sunny, but the evening had a chilly breeze.

Sharif's key in the lock at five past seven broke through her thoughts.

'You feel cold.' He took off his suit jacket and wrapped it around her, then led her inside. He flicked on the heating and sat beside her on the couch, drawing a blanket over both of them, her head on his shoulder.

She was grateful for the warmth, and she cuddled up to him, tucking her legs underneath her.

'So do you want to tell me? You don't have to, but if it would help, you have my undivided attention.' He took out his pager and switched it off and silenced his phone.

She told him the story Brian had shared with her, and he didn't interrupt, just let her speak. Once she'd finished, he remained quiet, absorbing what he'd heard. Panic set into Carmel. Maybe she was wrong and he was horrified by the circumstances of her conception on top of everything else and this was the last straw. Or maybe he was angry that she exerted Brian so much by asking him to tell her the story.

'Sharif, I'm sorry...' She had no idea how to reverse the last fifteen minutes, and she could feel her entire life crumbling away.

He turned to her, his dark eyes shining with unshed tears. 'Why are you sorry? What for? You have done nothing. Oh, Carmel, my love, I wish I could take some of this burden for you, I really do.' She'd never seen him so visibly upset. 'And poor Dolly, carrying that pain all these years when that...man got away with it. He wasn't content with destroying her youth, her innocence, but he ensured his poison remained potent by making sure you never got a happy home. I'm frustrated to hear he's dead – I would have liked to have confronted him. I'm not a violent man, Carmel, but I swear, I would like to hurt him. I would like for him to feel just a fraction of the pain he caused Dolly, and then you, my poor darling girl.' He held her tightly, soothingly kissing her hair and rubbing her back.

Relief flooded her senses. He was still there; he didn't reject her.

Well into the night, they talked, weighing up the various options. He thought maybe she should write a letter to Joe, outlining that he might be her father – she needn't say anything about the rape – and see if he would agree to a DNA test. She could then take it from there. If Joe was her father, then she could tell him the whole truth, but if he wasn't, then there was no point in destroying him with the knowledge of what his father did.

'Apart from Brian, she never told a soul. But now it's out. She's dead and so is Brian's father, so that changes it. She didn't want to tell Joe, and maybe I should respect her wishes, but then there's a chance that he's my father. Or even my half-brother. I don't know, Sharif, it's all so confusing.'

He stood up and made them both a gin and tonic. He returned to the sofa with the drinks and some snacks, placed them on the coffee table and took her hands in his. 'Let it sit for a while. This is so much to take in. Brian made a promise to Dolly that he wouldn't tell his brother, but as he said, he never made that promise about you. I know if it were me, even if I was happily married, I would want to know if a child of mine existed. But you'll have to sleep on it and decide. You'll know what to do – you just need to be patient with yourself. Take your time.'

They sipped their drinks in silence, the soft tones of Ella Fitzgerald playing on the sound system as Carmel planned her next move.

The choice was clear. She could delete the address from her phone, honour her mother's wish to never reveal to Joe McDaid the circumstances of her conception and let him live his life in peaceful ignorance. Or she could do what her heart was telling her, to make contact with the man who might be her father.

Sharif was right; the best thing to do was to let the idea settle for a while. Time would make it clear what she should do.

* * *

BRIAN WAS FADING ALL the time, but she popped in to see him most days. They didn't talk about Joe or Dolly; he was too weak for anything more than hello really. But she wanted him to know she was there. Tim spent most of every day with him, and she was careful to leave them alone together when he was there. Every moment was precious now.

Twenty days after Brian was admitted to Aashna House, Sharif got paged just as they were going to bed. Brian was weakening, and the night team had been instructed that if he deteriorated, Dr Khan was to be called. Carmel went with him.

Since arriving at Aashna, she had become comfortable with death. It was the strangest thing – it was so clearly a part of everyone's life but was shielded from most people as a very private, intimate thing. In Aashna, because it was a hospice, death was a daily occurrence, and while everyone was afforded the dignity, compassion and care they deserved, death wasn't spoken about in hushed terms or alluded to rather than named. She found it refreshing and liked to think it gave people a sense that there wasn't infinite time. The ever presence of death gave living an urgency she'd not experienced before.

They knocked gently and then entered. Brian was propped up on pillows, no drips or lines in or out. He seemed peaceful. A nurse was checking his chart.

'Thanks, I'll take over now,' Sharif whispered.

'His systolic BP is at sixty-six and his diastolic BP forty-four. Recurring apnoea and cyanosis of lower extremities.' She handed Sharif the chart and he looked at it.

'No liquids since early morning?'

'Nothing.'

'OK, thanks.'

The nurse left and Carmel sat beside Brian and held his hand. 'Should we call Tim?'

'No,' Sharif said calmly, checking Brian's vital signs. 'Brian told me three days ago he didn't want him to see it. They've said their goodbyes...'

'Hi, Brian.' Carmel leaned in to whisper in his ear. 'Carmel and Sharif are here now, and we're going to stay with you, OK? You just relax and we'll take care of you. You're not on your own.'

There was no way of knowing for sure, but there was a chance that he could hear them, so they sat either side of the bed and spoke gently and soothingly to him now and again. There was no need to administer any drugs. That time had passed. He'd had a morphine pump to manage the pain when he was drifting in and out of consciousness, but Sharif said he was one of the lucky ones; he seemed peaceful.

His eyes fluttered open for a moment. 'Dolly... Mam...' he whispered, his voice barely audible.

Suddenly, his face seemed to relax. He opened his eyes properly this time, and they seemed to be fixed on the top corner of the room. His eyes widened and brightened and his face melted into a radiant smile, as if he'd spotted someone he longed to see. The whole thing lasted mere seconds, and then he sighed deeply and was gone. Sharif stood and, after a few moments, checked Brian's pulse and then shut his eyes.

Carmel went to the window and opened it and covered the mirror with a towel.

'Why do you do that?' Sharif asked quietly. 'I've seen it in the Jewish culture but not in Christian families.'

'I don't know. It's just what we do in Ireland. We open the window to let the spirit free, I suppose, and we cover the mirrors so the soul of the departed doesn't get trapped inside. Superstition, I know, but he was Irish and so am I, so...' Carmel's voice cracked with emotion. Though she'd only known Brian a very short time, he had come to mean a lot to her.

Sharif gave her a hug and wiped her tears with his thumbs. 'I'm glad you met him and that he was able to tell you his story.'

'Me too.' She nodded and bent down to kiss Brian's forehead.

Sharif took Brian's medical notes and recorded the time of death, then went out to the office to make arrangements with the morgue.

Carmel looked down at the old man's face, all cares and pain gone. He looked peaceful.

'Thank you, Brian. Godspeed. And say hello to Dolly for me,' she whispered, patting the blankets around him.

The End.

I SINCERELY HOPE you enjoyed this book. If you would like to read on in the series and find out what happens next for Carmel and her family you can do so here in book 2, *The Future's Not Ours To See*:

https://geni.us/TheFuturesNotOursAL

If you would like to join my readers club, and get a free novel to download, please go to www.jeangrainger.com and sign up. It's 100% free and always will be.

Here is a sneak preview of the next instalment in the Carmel Sheehan Story.

AFTERWORD

This book came about, like most of my books, by chance. I was driving home one day when a woman called a radio talk show here in Ireland. The discussion that day was on the harrowing subject of the treatment of women and children in the institutions set up by the Catholic Church with the tacit approval of the Irish state between he years 1920 and 1990.

In a time of strict censure on how morality was perceived, women who became pregnant outside of marriage were systematically and cruelly imprisoned in places where they were expected to do hard manual labour for the duration of their pregnancy, for which they received no pay. Women and girls who were victims of sexual crime, incest or rape, had no recourse to the law. In fact, if they tried to leave these places they were returned by the Irish police, though they had committed no crime. Once their child was born, almost always without access to any pain relief, the children were adopted without the mother's consent. Needless to mention, the fathers of these children are never mentioned in the narrative, it was as if the women conceived all on their own.

It was a dark and awful time in our history and we need, as a nation to stand up and face it.

This woman on the radio that day was one such child and she spoke of her life in an institution. She was at pains to point out that while she didn't suffer the abuses we have come to expect from such places, she was neglected in the sense that nobody loved her. She was made to feel that she was a burden, a person who was a drain on the state. She described being raised without the love of parents, the companionship of siblings. She explained that nobody had ever taught her how to drive, do laundry, cook, how to buy a train ticket. The things our children pick up just by simply being part of a family, were a mystery to her. She spoke so eloquently about being thrown out into the world at eighteen, with nobody to help her and no idea how to exist. She described it as being as if everyone else had been to a school on how to live but she never went and so felt entirely adrift.

She had imagined what living in a family would be like, based on TV programmes, and had rushed into a marriage without the first person who offered, in the hope that finally she would belong somewhere. Unsurprisingly, it didn't work out.

I had to pull over and listen to her story, so touched was I by what she had to say.

Quite rightly, those innocent children and women who suffered so horrendously at the hands of people purporting to be doing the work of God must be heard and cared for and some effort made to lessen the pain, but this woman will never be part of that system. She wasn't a sex abuse victim, she wasn't forced into slave labour, she wasn't beaten, but she was not loved, or cared for or prepared for the adult world and that too is so very wrong.

That night the character of Carmel was born, and I hope I have managed to do that dark time justice.

ABOUT THE AUTHOR

Jean Grainger is a USA Today bestselling Irish author. She writes historical and contemporary Irish fiction and her work has very flatteringly been compared to the late great Maeve Binchy.

She lives in a stone cottage in Cork with her husband Diarmuid and the youngest two of her four children. The older two are finally self sufficient, productive members of society. There are a variety of animals there too, all led by two cute but clueless micro-dogs called Scrappy and Scoobi.

ALSO BY JEAN GRAINGER

Manufactured by Amazon.ca
Bolton, ON

37366992R00122